D1418181

McHenry's Last Shoot-Out

MC HENRY'S
LAST SHOOT-OUT

JAMES A. JANKE

AVALON BOOKS
THOMAS BOUREGY AND COMPANY, INC.
401 LAFAYETTE STREET
NEW YORK, NEW YORK 10003

156 1246

PRINTED IN THE UNITED STATES OF AMERICA
ON ACID-FREE PAPER
BY HADDON CRAFTSMEN, SCRANTON, PENNSYLVANIA

Dedicated to
Andrew and Laura

Chapter One

"EXCUSE me, sir," the young woman said pleasantly. "Are you headed for Flagstaff too?"

Jason McHenry's head bobbed about as the stage-coach bounced over the rough desert road. He realized that she was probably trying to make conversation to make the endless miles go faster, but in his somber mood he didn't feel much like talking to anyone, not even to the five people—a woman and four men—sharing the cramped vehicle with him. And, anyhow, the heat was making him drowsy.

Still, he had to admit that the beauty of the woman across from him was a definite tonic to his troubled mind. How old was she? Eighteen, maybe younger. She wore an attractive blue dress with vertical white stripes that accentuated a slim and comely figure. Waves of red-brown hair cascaded from under a wide-brimmed hat. Dark-brown eyes looked at him pleasantly from a pretty face with high cheekbones and a slim nose and an almost-white complexion. How she managed to maintain that fashionable shade of paleness

1

in the burning sun of Arizona amazed McHenry. And she didn't seem the least bothered by the heat.

So he stopped staring out the stage window and answered her. "Actually, I'm headed for Chicago," he said.

"Oh? That's a very long journey from here. Are you going to visit someone in Chicago?"

McHenry shook his head. "Nope. Moving there permanent."

The middle-aged male companion of the young lady blurted, "Chicago? What on earth is a man like you moving to Chicago for?"

McHenry's eyes narrowed at what sounded like an insult. The man was wearing shiny brown shoes and a heavy pin-striped suit with a vest, which must have felt like an oven on a day like today. McHenry had doffed his jacket and rolled up his shirtsleeves, but the sweat still made the back of his shirt stick to the coach. The breeze coming in the window didn't help at all, because it was hot and dusty.

The young woman playfully slapped the man on his wrist. "Father, that didn't sound polite," she scolded with a smile.

"No offense intended, sir," her father said quickly. "In fact, I meant it as a compliment. You look like you belong here." He gestured toward McHenry, who wore battered boots, rough trousers, a shirt, and a leather vest that looked like it had been through a cattle stampede. "A young man like you—why, you fit this land. I'd say you're quite an asset here."

The girl laughed and pointed to herself as she continued looking at McHenry. "Sir, I don't think we look like *we* fit here, do we?"

McHenry smiled. "Ma'am, you'd fit perfectly anywhere."

She smiled self-consciously and lowered her a head a trifle. "Thank you, sir," she said softly. "My name is Peggy Winslow."

McHenry touched the brim of his dusty hat. "A pleasure to meet you, ma'am. I'm Jason McHenry."

Peggy pointed to her father. "This is my father, Eli Winslow."

Winslow reached over and extended a hand. "Pleased to meet you, Mr. McHenry."

McHenry stretched to shake the offered hand. "Mr. Winslow."

The man next to McHenry in the middle spoke for the first time: "But you're right, Mr. Winslow. He belongs here, not in Chicago. He's just turned out to be a quitter."

McHenry turned to the man. "Mitch, I oughta bust your face in for that. It's not like I didn't try."

Peggy said, "You two seem to know each other. I thought that might be so, from the few words you'd exchanged before."

"Jason's not the talkative kind, especially now," Mitch explained.

"Oh?"

"I ranch near Jason," Mitch added, jerking a thumb toward McHenry. "Or I did until the young fool sold out to the rancher north of him and decided to run away to—"

"Shut up, Mitch," McHenry said. "I'm not running away. I just decided to do something different."

Uncomfortable, Peggy cleared her throat and looked at Mitch. "And you are . . . ?"

Mitch tipped his hat. "Mitchell Dragseth, miss," he said. "At your service. And Flagstaff is where I'm headed. To buy me some machinery. Gonna try makin' my own lumber."

"Machinery?" Peggy turned to her father. "My father loves machinery. He's with the railroad."

Winslow leaned forward and shook hands with Mitch. "Pleased to meet you, Mr. Dragseth."

"Oh, folks just call me Mitch," Mitch said. "Railroad, huh? We could use a railroad through here. Link us to markets all over the country."

"Well, Mitch, that's just the kind of thing I'm doing on these trips—trying to find where economic growth could be the fastest, where a railroad would be most profitable. I brought my daughter along this time to show her what she was missing in San Francisco."

On the other end of McHenry's seat sat a young cavalry officer, and he spoke up: "Heading back to California after you reach Flagstaff, Mr. Winslow?"

"No, we're going all the way to Santa Fe before we turn back," Peggy told him.

"Really?" the officer said brightly. "That's wonderful. I'm headed for Washington, so we'll be riding together all the way to Santa Fe. My name's Bradley Falwell. Lieutenant Bradley Falwell."

Peggy smiled. "Pleased to meet you, sir."

"Going to give a report to the War Department in Washington?" Winslow asked. "I hope you mention that we can use more help with these Apaches. No doubt this used to be their land, but progress is progress."

"I expect my experience out here fighting the Apache will be invaluable to them in Washington, Mr. Winslow."

McHenry looked at the lieutenant in cynical amusement. The lieutenant's uniform looked fairly new, with none of the fraying that he had seen on so many of the experienced officers out in this desert country. The brass buttons on Falwell's tunic still glistened, and the yellow stripe on his trouser leg had not yet faded to dull gold. Just how much experience fighting Indians could Falwell have had? First, he didn't look much older than Peggy, and second, the U.S. Cavalry usually spent their time chasing Apaches but never catching and fighting them. You usually got a chance to fight Apaches only when they decided to attack you, as they did with ranchers who had seized their sacred lands and streams. McHenry figured he'd been in more fights

with the Apaches than Falwell had. And even then he
had hardly seen the Apaches he was fighting. They
were like ghosts.

"I've been appointed to a staff position there," Falwell went on.

"Really?" Winslow said. "Don't often hear about
frontier officers winding up in Washington."

Falwell smiled. "My uncle is Senator Falwell from
New York."

"Ah, yes," Winslow acknowledged, a knowing
smile on his face. "A strong supporter of our railroad,
in fact." *For a price, the greedy bandit.*

On the other side of Winslow, a potbellied man in
a rumpled brown suit had been dozing. He took this
opportunity to belch loudly. He looked about, a bit
embarrassed, but not much.

"And you, sir?" Falwell asked. His voice was dis-
approving.

"Totten," the man said. "Josiah Totten. Mining
equipment. And the mines could use a railroad too."

Peggy turned to McHenry. "With all this economic
potential, why are you moving to Chicago?"

Mitch snorted. "To work in the stockyards, if you
can believe that."

"I've got an uncle too," McHenry said. "But he's
not a senator."

Falwell shot a suspicious glance in McHenry's direction. Peggy noticed it and frowned. "But you're a
rancher like Mr. Dragseth here, aren't you?"

"Please," Mitch said, holding up a hand. "Mitch, just Mitch."

Peggy smiled. "Mitch."

"He's a good rancher too, miss," Mitch said. "One of the best. Could have made a go of it too, if he'd stuck it out a little longer."

"How long does it take, Mitch?" McHenry said. "I tried for seven years—seven years of drought and heat and dust and sickness and Apaches and bandits. Grass burned up, cows run off by Apaches or rustlers, brother got sick and died, hired hands left or got killed by Apaches. I tried, but I'm just worn out."

"You never learned to love the land, Jason," Mitch said. "It was never home to you. As for me, I'll never leave my place no matter how much heat or how many Apaches."

"All you'll get for your work," McHenry said, "is an early grave."

"Yeah? But at least I'll be home on my own land. My house. What do you have to show for your seven years of work? No home, just a few gold coins in your pack. Why, you even sold your saddle. How could you do that? Just don't seem right."

McHenry looked out the window again and pulled his hat lower over his eyes. "I won't need a saddle in Chicago." He folded his arms and made a point of staring at sagebrush.

"You can still change your mind. Casey said he'd

be glad to sell the ranch right back to you for what he paid you for it.''

''Mostly he paid the bank,'' McHenry said. ''I owed them most of what the ranch was worth.''

Mitch sighed. ''Well, get your last look at the best country in the world, Jason. Nothin' like this in Chicago.'' He said the name of the city with derision.

''No, but there aren't any Apaches there, either.''

''The Army will soon have the Apaches under control,'' Falwell said.

Mitch laughed. ''The only way to control 'em is to kill 'em. I hear that they've vowed to their ancestors that they'll recapture and purify these lands.''

''But aren't they all men too, just like you?'' Peggy asked.

Mitch just stared at her, and even McHenry turned back to look. Totten buried his head in disgust against the wall of the stage and decided to try to go back to sleep. Falwell blinked several times.

Winslow raised an eyebrow and turned to his daughter. ''I daresay they don't think that at all, my dear,'' he said.

The stagecoach came to a sudden stop, harness and tack rattling, brake squealing, the driver cursing, the passengers lurching forward. McHenry glanced outside. They were in the middle of nowhere. He stuck his head out the window. ''Hey, driver! Why are we stopping here?''

"We got big trouble up ahead, mister!" the driver answered.

Instinctively, McHenry's right hand slipped down to his pistol in its holster strapped to his hip.

"Oh, dear," Peggy said. Her hand touched her lips.

"What kind of trouble?" McHenry called out to the driver.

"Come out and see for yourself," the driver answered.

McHenry didn't like the sound of that. If a horse had simply slipped a harness, the driver could have said so. McHenry opened the stagecoach door and hopped out. The other passengers followed quickly, Mitch first.

Falwell helped Peggy out. "Thank you, Lieutenant," she said smiling.

"You're welcome, Miss Winslow."

McHenry looked up at the driver. He was still sitting in place, the reins held tightly in his hands. He was looking off into the distance straight ahead. The shotgun guard had climbed on top of the coach and was squinting in the same direction.

McHenry followed their stare, but he saw nothing. He quickly scanned the horizon all around. They were surrounded by low hills and desert for miles, and well beyond that in the east were mesas and canyons. There wasn't a tuft of parched grass or a sagebrush clump more than two feet high in any direction, though there was plenty of the sagebrush in many places. It was as if they were adrift in a vast sea of yellow, tan, and gray, all shimmering in late-afternoon summer heat.

McHenry was confused. "Just what am I supposed to be seeing, driver?" he asked.

"It's what you don't see anymore," the driver told him.

"The stage station's been burned," the shotgun guard added. "You can just see a little smoke risin' from where it used to be. Straight ahead."

McHenry's ears twitched. He heard Peggy gasp. Totten muttered something and wiped his lips. He climbed back into the stagecoach.

"Apaches," Falwell said.

"Apaches is right," Mitch agreed. His hand slipped to the butt of his pistol in its holster.

The driver said to his helper, "Billy, your eyes are sharper than mine. See any of 'em?"

"Nope," Billy answered. He made a slow, complete circle on top of the stagecoach, shielding his eyes from the sun low in the sky. "Nothin', Al," he reported.

McHenry noticed that Billy was probably younger than Peggy. But the Winchester he carried was all grown up.

"Humph," Al said. He kept staring toward the burned-out station.

McHenry settled the holster on his hip, drew the pistol, and flipped open the loading gate. He knew perfectly well that each chamber was loaded, but he went through the check, anyway. It gave him a feeling of security that he knew at the same time was an illusion. He noticed that Mitch was also checking his pistol. Winslow and the lieutenant were not wearing pistols.

"Billy," McHenry said, "I've got a Winchester in my roll up there. Toss it down. And my box of cartridges in the pack."

"You bet," Billy replied eagerly. He pulled the carbine from the bedroll and tossed it down to McHenry. Then he rummaged through McHenry's small pack of belongings, found a box of cartridges, and tossed that down too.

"Thanks," McHenry said. He turned to Mitch. "You bring a rifle?" The Apaches would have rifles, and a pistol wasn't much good until you got real close, if they let you.

Mitch shook his head. His brow was furrowed. "No, because I thought they'd be more likely to need it at home. Ain't heard of Apaches in this direction for years."

"Me, neither. Maybe the last few settlements of whites were more than they could take."

"Driver," Falwell said, "I have a sidearm in my trunk in the rear boot."

"Right." Al climbed down from the top of the coach and walked to the rear. He started undoing the tarp in back.

McHenry and Mitch started forward slowly. McHenry slipped cartridges from the box into the Winchester's magazine through the loading gate while they walked. They reached the leader span of horses. McHenry patted the horse on the neck, and the horse whickered and turned to look at him. The animal was breathing hard and rapidly, and his flanks were wet.

"These horses are beat," McHenry told Mitch. "This heat is killing them."

"Well, there won't be any fresh ones at the station this time," Mitch said. "The Apaches will have run off with 'em."

Al joined them, saying, "But at least there's still water at the station. You can see my horses are worn out. They need water bad, so we gotta go on down there, no matter if it is burned." He pointed to McHenry's Winchester. "McHenry, you suppose—"

McHenry nodded. "I'll ride on top with this."

"Much obliged. Billy's a good shot, but two of you will be a lot better. Just in case."

"Right," McHenry said. "Well, let's go have a look."

They walked back. McHenry climbed atop the stage-coach and settled in amid the baggage. The other passengers got back into the coach. Mitch sat at a rear window and looked forward, and Falwell sat on the other end of the seat at that window. Both of them held their pistols in their laps. The other three passengers sat on the seat opposite.

"Heeyah!" Al shouted. He snapped the reins and the tired horses started off.

The coach rode easily on the slight downhill slope, and Al kept the team at a moderate pace until they got within about half a mile of the station. Then he slowed the team and they walked the rest of the way. Al kept squinting from the station ruins to the sagebrush on either side of the road. He was ready to bolt the horses at the first sign of an Apache.

The station had been leveled. The wooden parts of the building had burned away, leaving low adobe walls and foundations about three feet high. The stable had crumbled to charred ruins, and even part of the corral fence had been pulled down. Wisps of smoke drifted up from the wreckage of the station.

Al brought the team to a halt in front of the station. He set the brake, secured the reins to the brake handle, pulled a Winchester carbine from the front boot, and climbed down. As he headed slowly for the ruins, he told Billy, "You stay up there and keep your eyes open."

"Right," Billy said.

McHenry said to Al from on top of the stagecoach, "I'll come with you."

"I'll come too," Mitch said.

As they strode after Al, Falwell, Peggy, and Winslow disembarked but clustered near the stage. Totten stayed in the coach. Falwell remained close to Peggy, keeping his pistol in hand but dangling it at his side.

"This probably happened yesterday," McHenry remarked, looking around. "The fire's pretty well burned out." Then he scanned the surrounding desert. "I doubt the Apaches are nearby. They don't like to stick around after a raid."

"Maybe, maybe not," Al said. "Maybe they're waitin' to see who comes to investigate. Or maybe they've been waitin' for this stage."

McHenry shook his head. "Not like them. Did they have some reason to expect us?"

Al shrugged. "Apaches sure don't read schedules, but if they've been around here for long, they'd know that a stage comes through every couple of days."

"Who lived here?" Mitch asked.

"Bob Harrington and his boys, Austin and Jeremy. That's what I'm looking for—their bodies. I hate to say such a thing, but I hope I find their bodies."

The other two men nodded. They knew what the alternatives were. "Any womenfolk?" Mitch asked cautiously.

Al shook his head. "Emma caught a fever a couple of years ago. Her grave's in the back."

They circled all the way around the station and even examined the stable. They spread out and walked the perimeter of the station, searching the sagebrush.

"Nothin'." Al let his carbine droop.

"I was hopin' we'd find 'em," Mitch said. "Guess maybe the Apaches carried 'em off."

The three men looked at one another, but not one of them spoke of what was running through his mind, for the pictures were unspeakable.

Al ran a hand over his face to wipe off the perspiration and dirt. "I'm goin' over to the well to get water for the horses," he said. "We'll have to give 'em a good rest before we do anything else."

McHenry and Mitch watched him go. They also glanced at the other people. Totten was still in the stagecoach. Winslow had gone to talk to Al as he neared the well. Billy stood on top of the coach, and Falwell stuck close to Peggy.

"Wish she hadn't seen this," McHenry said.

"Yeah," Mitch agreed. "Guess her pa had her see more than he wanted her to see."

Al shouted suddenly. McHenry and Mitch saw him standing at the side of the well, looking down into it. Winslow was looking down into the well too. He had a hand over his mouth.

"The Harringtons, I'll bet," McHenry said. "Come on."

He and Mitch jogged over to the well. They felt compelled to look down even though they knew they wouldn't like what they would see. They just had to know.

Enough light reached into the well for them to see a bloated, mutilated body floating face-up in the dark water.

"It's Bob," Al said. "At least I think it's Bob."

"And the boys?" McHenry asked with a grimace. "Do you see them? I think there's only one body down there."

Al shook his head. "Just looks like Bob alone."

"How old were the boys?" Mitch asked.

Al shrugged. "Don't know exactly. 'Round ten or so." He used a hand to measure off a height against his own chest. "About so high."

"The Apaches might have taken them along to adopt," McHenry said.

Mitch shook his head just once. "Seems a little old to me. You've never had a ten-year-old boy, Jason."

Winslow's face was ashen. "This is horrible. We must do something immediately. Those boys have to be found."

The three men at the well just looked at him.

"Like what?" Mitch snapped angrily. He shot a glance over at the stagecoach. "That's a job the Army should be doin'."

"You mean Lieutenant Falwell?" Winslow asked.

Mitch snorted. "That puppy wouldn't scare an Apache squaw, much less a whole raidin' party. There's nothing we can do." He spit into the dirt.

McHenry patted him on the shoulder and said, "You're right." Then he turned to Al. "Do we go on or do we go back? Is the next station a small one too?"

Al took a deep breath and let it out slowly. "The next station is just like this one, and there's a good chance it's been raided too. It would be mighty temptin'. I think we should go back, but the horses are dead on their feet and the water's no good anymore. We just have to give 'em some rest. And it's almost dusk already. We'll head back in the mornin'.''

McHenry nodded. ''Makes sense to me. And if the Apaches are watching us, they might not want to stick around till tomorrow to hit us. They could clear out tonight.''

Billy yelled from the top of the stage, ''Al, company's comin'!'' He lifted his Winchester and pointed east.

The four men at the well followed his pointing. Coming slowly through the sagebrush, three riders were heading in the direction of the station. McHenry and Al got good grips on their Winchesters.

''Those men don't look like Apaches,'' Winslow said, squinting.

''Bandits,'' McHenry suggested.

''Mexicans, from the looks of 'em,'' Mitch said. ''Every one a cutthroat and lookin' for booty north of the border, just like the Apaches. No better.''

McHenry turned to Winslow. ''Sir, you'd better get your daughter out of sight. Take her around behind the stable. The adobe walls are still tall enough to hide a couple of people there.''

Al nodded slowly. ''I think that's a real good idea, Mr. Winslow. These three will probably just ride off when they see how many we are, but that pretty daughter of yours is too temptin' a treasure to pass up. They're far enough away at the moment, and they might not have seen her yet.''

Winslow's jaw clenched. "I understand." He turned quickly and strode toward the stage.

Al called toward the stage, "Billy, get down from there."

Billy jumped right off the top of the stage and rolled on the ground. He got to his feet quickly and scampered behind the coach. He stood there using the stage as a shield, watching the three horsemen approach.

"Fellas," McHenry said, "I suggest we spread out so's to cover them from a wide angle. Mitch, you stay here by the well. If it comes to a shoot-out, they'll go for our carbines first and you can use the well wall to steady that Colt of yours and maybe get a couple of them while we keep them busy."

The other two men agreed and they spread out. Mitch leaned casually against the well. McHenry sauntered over to a spot near the corral. Al went to the head of his horses. There really was no cover for either McHenry or Al, but the approaching bandits didn't have any cover, either.

McHenry checked the stage, but could see no sign of Peggy or Winslow. Totten must have been crouching down in the stage, because McHenry couldn't see him through the windows. Falwell stood near the stage-coach door. His gun hand drooped at his side, but McHenry thought the pistol was already cocked. All McHenry could see of Billy were his boots and legs on the other side of the stagecoach.

The three horsemen stopped just short of effective pistol range. McHenry didn't like that.

"*Buenos días, amigos,*" the leader called.

"Howdy," Al answered. "Where you men headed?"

The leader looked surprised. "*Aquí,*" he said. "We come here. Right here." He pointed with a finger to the spot they stood on.

"What's your business?" Al asked.

The leader waved a hand around toward the ruins of the station. "You have trouble, no? Maybe we help."

"Don't need any help," McHenry put in.

"You not worried about Apaches?" the bandit leader asked. "They burn this place. They still around too. Maybe they come after you."

"We can handle them," McHenry called.

He watched the Mexican leader. The man stopped talking and sat motionless. McHenry was sure the man was calculating odds. There were three of the bandits, whose horses would jump and spoil the their aim if shooting started. But the three bandits would be facing five men steady on their feet with three carbines and two pistols among them. Who would call that good odds?

"I think maybe the three of you should just ride on," McHenry said.

"Aren't you worried about the Apaches yourself?" Al added.

The leader turned his gaze on Al. "No, señor," he said slowly. "I not worried."

McHenry felt uneasy. This didn't seem to be going right. The bandit seemed to be waiting for something. The other two horsemen seemed downright calm and relaxed.

Finally the leader spoke again. "We are not just three, amigos," he said. He pointed past McHenry.

McHenry turned and his ears twitched again. There were eight more horsemen in a line slowly coming up through the sagebrush from the west, with the blinding sun behind them. McHenry cursed himself. They'd been tricked.

Mitch started to back around the well, but then stopped. He knew the well would be no cover now. And Billy started to edge around the side of the stagecoach. He, too, knew that he was completely exposed now.

The eight horsemen halted. The bandit leader leaned forward on the pommel of his saddle. "You carry gold with you, señor driver?" he asked.

"No, no gold," Al answered. "Just passengers."

"Hm. Maybe passengers carry gold?"

"Nope."

McHenry thought about the pitiful number of gold coins in the small pouch in his pack on top of the stagecoach. Now he wished he had just stuffed the coins in his pocket. Somehow, that would have seemed safer. But he really knew it didn't matter.

The Mexican fell silent again. McHenry could tell he was still calculating. No man is in a hurry to die. The odds were eleven to five now, but McHenry figured that he and the others still did not look like easy pickings. And the leader knew he would be the first one shot at. That was how he kept his leadership—by leading, even into danger.

The Mexican doffed his sombrero. "Well, adios, amigos," he said. He whistled and started to turn his horse.

McHenry let out a sigh of relief.

Then Peggy screamed.

Everyone spun around. Three bandits were dragging Peggy and Winslow from their hiding place behind the adobe wall. One had lifted Peggy clear off the ground by throwing an arm around her waist. He had a big smile on his face and was jabbering wildly. Two Mexicans were manhandling Winslow, who struggled hard but was really no match for the tough outlaws.

McHenry jerked his head around to look at the bandit leader. The man was now standing upright in his stirrups, his mouth agape. The other two outlaws with him were pointing toward Peggy and smiling and exclaiming to their leader.

Without moving another muscle, still standing in the stirrups with his mouth open, the bandit's eyes shifted toward McHenry looking up at him. Peggy had tipped the calculation the other way. The Mexican went for his gun.

Everyone else followed. McHenry fired his carbine from his hip. He got off three quick shots at the leader, but the man's bouncing horse made every bullet miss.

Al's carbine was closer, and the nearest outlaw was slammed from his horse. The third man opened up on Mitch behind the well, and Mitch returned the fire.

The eight outlaws on the other side of the station charged in a thunder of hooves. They opened up on Billy behind the stagecoach. Billy gave as good as he got. He plucked two of the bandits from their saddles before the fusillade of bullets tore into his body and dropped him to the ground. A hail of bullets thudded into the back of the stagecoach, and the stage horses, terrified at the sudden crash of gunfire, bolted despite the brake.

Peggy screamed again as the bandit dropped her and went for his pistol. McHenry turned toward her screams and dropped to one knee. He snapped the carbine to his shoulder, but before he could fire, Falwell put two big slugs into the bandit's chest and knocked him flat. The lieutenant's third bullet missed his next target, but the fourth bullet caught a second bandit in the head just as the man ducked for the adobe wall. Falwell might even have gotten the third Mexican, except the large hub of the rear wheel of the rushing stagecoach smashed into Falwell's leg and spun him around to topple over on the ground.

The third outlaw took a shot at Winslow, but he missed because the railroad man took a flying leap to land on top of his daughter. McHenry shifted his aim and fired off a quick shot. The bullet slammed into the bandit's arm and jerked him around. McHenry's second bullet hit him squarely in the chest and knocked him over a low wall.

Satisfied that Peggy was safe for the moment, McHenry whirled around again. The bandit leader and the remaining horseman with him were racing off. Al and Mitch had turned and were firing at the bandits still charging from the west. McHenry joined in, levering in new cartridges and firing as fast as he could. When the carbine was empty, he drew his pistol and started using that.

The heavy fire from the three of them halted the rush of the outlaws. They milled about and gestured toward their leader who was heading off in a cloud of dust. Another man pitched from his saddle. The rest turned and raced toward the south, then veered around in a wide circle to chase after their leader.

The six stagecoach horses galloped after the bandit leader too, and the stagecoach, with its brake smoking, disappeared in a cloud of dust.

Chapter Two

FORLORNLY McHenry, Mitch, and Al watched the receding cloud of dust.

"Who'd have thought those horses could run like that, tired as they are?" Mitch said.

"That supposed to be funny?" Al asked angrily.

"No!" Mitch admitted. "It ain't funny at all."

"You know," McHenry said, "I think Totten is still on the stage." *And so is my gold*, he felt like adding.

Mitch shook his head slowly. "They'll kill him first thing. Guess that was the wrong place to hide."

McHenry shrugged. "Without the stagecoach, we aren't in very good shape ourselves."

Neither of the other two men argued with that statement.

"I gotta check on Billy," Al said.

All three men headed back toward where the stagecoach had been sitting. On the way they passed Falwell, lying flat on his back with Peggy and Winslow attending to him. Peggy was cradling his head and brush-

ing hair back from his forehead. McHenry thought that
a broken leg was probably worth that kind of treatment.

Winslow was bending over Falwell's leg. "That
hurt?" he asked as he touched it gently.

Falwell grimaced. "Some, Mr. Winslow, some."

A lot is more like it, McHenry thought from the look
on Falwell's face.

Winslow stood up slowly. "I don't think it's broken,
Lieutenant. You were lucky."

"I was lucky too, Lieutenant," Peggy said. "You
saved my life."

McHenry felt like mentioning that *he* had shot the
third bandit, but he thought that that would sound child-
ish. "I saw that shooting you did, Lieutenant," he said
instead. "That was superb. With a pistol at that distance, no less." Though Falwell lacked experience, he
was a crack shot.

Falwell just shrugged.

McHenry looked at Winslow. "You were brave to
throw yourself on top of your daughter like that."

Winslow looked at him in puzzlement. "She might
have gotten shot!"

"They wouldn't have shot her on purpose."

"A stray bullet wouldn't know who it was hitting,"
Winslow pointed out.

"No, but. . . ." McHenry didn't know what he was
trying to say. Maybe that he wished he loved someone
enough to throw himself without hesitation in the line
of fire to protect her.

Winslow smiled a little. "But thanks for the compliment."

McHenry just nodded. Then he turned and walked over to where Mitch and Al were standing over Billy. Al had taken off his hat and was holding it in front with both hands rolling up the brim.

"He just turned sixteen two months ago," Al said. "What am I gonna tell his ma and pa? How am I gonna face 'em?"

"Boys gotta grow up fast out here." Mitch sighed. "And some die awful young." There was pain in his voice.

"Suppose there's a shovel still around?" McHenry asked. "At least, Al, you could say we gave him a decent burial."

Al nodded. "Yeah, that might help."

"But first," McHenry said, "we have to catch that horse over there."

The others looked up sharply. Indeed, a single horse was standing in the sagebrush off to the west. Its rider lay dead in the sagebrush nearby.

"It's only one," McHenry said, "but even one is a lot better than none."

"That's for sure," Al agreed. "But do you suppose he's wounded? Why's he still here? All the others ran off."

"Let's go find out," Mitch said. "Spread out so we don't spook him."

The three men fanned out and surrounded the horse

at a distance and then closed in on him. The horse did try to shy away, but McHenry managed to grab his trailing reins. They checked the animal. He had not been wounded in the gunfight, and maybe he was just particularly stupid for a horse. They brought him back to the station and hitched him to the corral fence.

Falwell was up and had his pistol tucked into his tunic belt. He limped badly, and Peggy and Winslow helped support him. The three of them joined the men standing next to the horse.

Al spoke first: "The way I see it, one of us has to ride back to the last town for help."

"Can't we all just sit here and wait for the next stage?" Peggy asked.

Al shook his head. "We don't know how long before another stage will come through."

"But isn't there a schedule?" Winslow asked.

"When news of these Apaches gets out, the stage will stop runnin' for a while. It could be a couple of weeks."

"I see." Winslow took his daughter's hand and squeezed it.

"And we got no food and no water and no shade," Al added.

"Couldn't we do some hunting?" Winslow asked.

"Not with those bandits and maybe Apaches out there," McHenry said.

"Ah, yes." Winslow grimaced. "No hunting. But

are the bandits likely to come back? I mean, you gentlemen gave them a pretty good thrashing, as I see it.''

"We have something they want," McHenry reminded him.

Peggy seemed to shrink. Winslow put an arm around her and asked, ''And the Apaches?''

"Apaches don't like to stay in one place too long, Mr. Winslow," Mitch said. "Gives the Army a chance to find 'em. No matter what the prize," he went on, shifting his eyes toward Peggy, "they'll leave shortly if they haven't already. They just don't like to take chances. Maybe this isn't their home and they were just up here raidin'."

"But those bandits aren't so prudent," McHenry observed. "They'll be back."

"So we need help in a big hurry." Al looked off into the distance. "And the way I see it, that'll mean two days at the minimum. One day to get to town and another day at least to get help back here. And that's if the town gets a posse together. They're more likely to telegraph Fort Johnson."

"And that will mean another day, probably two," McHenry said.

"Three days without food and water?" Winslow groaned. "And Apaches and bandits all around us." He gave his daughter a desperate hug. "My dear, I'm so sorry I got you into this."

Peggy hugged her father back. "You didn't know it would happen, Father. We'll make it."

McHenry saw from the look on Winslow's face that he wasn't convinced.

Falwell made a weak smile. "There's another possibility. There is an Army patrol south of here, probably only a half day's ride."

"How do you know that?" McHenry asked.

"We had heard rumors of an Apache raiding party heading in this direction, and we were trying to head them off if it were true."

"Wish the Army would have told us," Al growled.

"They were just rumors."

"Seems the rumors were true," McHenry said.

Falwell turned to him. "But usually they aren't. We would have the countryside in a continuous uproar if we circulated every rumor we hear."

"I don't care about all that!" Winslow snapped. "I just want to know how to get my daughter to safety."

"But how would you ever find a patrol, even if you know it's down there somewhere?" McHenry asked Falwell. "It's a big country."

"Unless something happens, the patrol will stick to a schedule. Tonight, this very night, they should be camping near Beartooth Butte."

McHenry snorted. "A schedule? No wonder the Army can't catch the Apaches. Apaches don't keep schedules."

Falwell glared at him. "Well, this schedule might just save your neck, Mr. McHenry."

"But what if something has happened and the patrol

isn't there?'' Winslow asked. "Won't that have wasted another day or more?''

Falwell shook his head. "No. If the patrol isn't there, you could ride on south to Mesa City and telegraph Fort Johnson from there.''

"I'll bet Mesa City is even closer than goin' back the way we came,'' Mitch said.

Falwell nodded vigorously.

"But who goes?'' Winslow asked. "It will have to be one of you gentlemen. I won't leave my daughter.''

"Nor will I,'' Falwell announced. "I think that's my duty.''

McHenry wondered how he figured that, but after recalling the way the lieutenant had shot the two bandits, he preferred that Falwell stay.

"Well,'' Al drawled, "I hate to say it, but I don't know where this Beartooth Butte is. I've been to Mesa City, but not from this direction.''

"Could you draw me a map?'' McHenry asked Falwell. "I'll go.''

Mitch raised a hand. "Wait a minute. I don't need a map.''

McHenry looked skeptically at Mitch. "I've never before seen you more than fifty miles away from your ranch.''

Mitch laughed. "You forget that I was once your age and used to roam all over this country. I could find Beartooth Butte in the dark.''

"That's even better,'' Falwell said. "Mitch, you

have to be the one to go. Tonight. Soon as it gets dark.''

"Mitch, no one's waiting for me back home," McHenry pointed out.

"I'll be no safer here than out there," Mitch said.

McHenry had to admit that that might be true. A single man on a horse might be safer than a whole bunch of people afoot. He could make a run for it, but they couldn't. And he couldn't argue with the logic of sending a man who knew where he was going.

"Well, at least you'll be able to take a rifle with you," McHenry said to Mitch. "There are plenty of guns lying around now."

Mitch nodded. "I'll find that patrol, don't you worry. And I'll lead 'em back here as fast as I can."

"Not here," Al said. "We can't stay here."

Winslow frowned. "There's no stagecoach. We can't go anywhere."

"Let's head back ourselves," Al said. "Start tonight. Be gone before the bandits return tomorrow."

"You mean walk?" Winslow asked in astonishment. "Why? Wouldn't this be a better place to fight them off? You must have killed half of them already."

McHenry nodded. "I see what Al's getting at. We don't know how many bandits there really are. Besides, Billy's dead and Mitch will be gone. Can you shoot a gun, Mr. Winslow?"

"I'll do what I have to," he said firmly.

"Yeah, but can you hit anything?" Mitch asked.

"Well. . . ."

McHenry went on, "I don't think the bandits will come back until tomorrow morning. They'll go through the stagecoach for one thing. And they can't expect that we'll be going anywhere."

"But—"

"This isn't going to be a good place to defend," Falwell pointed out. "We can't hide in the ashes and ruins. We're exposed on all sides out in the open, but they'll have all that brush to conceal themselves. Those bandits won't come riding in tomorrow the way they did today."

"But how far could we get?" Winslow asked. "Do you expect my daughter to march down the road? And we'll be in the open, exposed to attack. Not to mention the sun frying our brains."

"We'll travel at night," McHenry said. "It'll be cool."

"And we'll hole up in the first good place we find. With shade and good cover," Al assured Winslow.

"But we still wouldn't have any water," Winslow pointed out.

McHenry nodded again. "Good point, Mr. Winslow. And I agree we wouldn't get far. They would catch up to us very quickly. We could be trapped for days without water."

"Jason," Mitch said, "I can't figure out which side of this argument you're on."

"Do you mean we should walk to the next station

even if the Apaches haven't burned it?'' Al asked. ''That sounds like a worse idea to me.''

McHenry shook his head. ''I don't think that's what we should do, either. We should go after the bandits.''

Al squinted at McHenry. ''You gone loco?''

''That's the last thing they'll expect us to do,'' McHenry said. ''Particularly with a woman with us. And they'll have water and food and horses. And ammunition.''

Falwell slapped his good leg. ''By golly, McHenry, I like it.''

McHenry waved a hand toward the growing darkness. ''There's some moon tonight, and the stage's wheel tracks ought to be easy to follow. I don't think the bandits will go far at all. They intend to come back tomorrow morning, and they don't expect us to be going anywhere. Why, they could be camped right over that hill there.''

''Gentlemen,'' Falwell said, ''McHenry is right. Attack. Tonight. Surprise will be on our side. We have plenty of weapons now and could probably overtake them on foot in a couple of hours.'' He glanced at Peggy. ''Even with Miss Winslow along.''

''This—this is preposterous,'' Winslow insisted. He clutched his daughter more tightly.

''So is staying here, Mr. Winslow,'' McHenry said.

''And what if we don't catch up to the bandits?'' Winslow asked. ''What then? What if there are Apaches out there?''

"Whatever we choose to do is going to be risky," McHenry pointed out. "Staying here is risky, heading back to town is risky, and attacking the bandits is risky. But the last choice is our best hope."

"And what if we wind up wandering around those canyons for days?" Winslow asked. "Maybe no bandits and no Apaches, but no food either, and no water, and no hope."

"At least we'll have shade from the sun for part of the time," McHenry said. "And we might just find us some water too. When Mitch gets back, he can follow us."

"And what if," Winslow said, sighing deeply, "Mitch doesn't make it?"

"I'll make it," Mitch insisted. "Don't worry."

"You mean," Peggy said, speaking for the first time, "that you intend to just go out and murder a bunch of men in their sleep?"

"It won't be murder, Miss Winslow." Falwell clenched a hand in anger. "These are horrible men, I assure you. There's not a one of them that wouldn't hang if he were captured by the law."

"Would you prefer that we wake them up before we shoot them?" McHenry asked. "It's them or us."

Winslow shook his head as if to clear it. "This is all ghastly."

"The best defense is often an offense, Mr. Winslow," Falwell said.

"Do you have a better suggestion, Mr. Winslow?" McHenry asked.

Winslow shook his head. He sighed. "No, I don't."

Mitch hoisted himself into the saddle of the captured horse. He patted the animal on the neck. "Seems like a steady fellow," he said.

Standing next to the horse, McHenry grinned. "So are you, Mitch."

Mitch laughed. He gathered the reins up tightly and looked around at the black sky filling up with stars. "Some moon tonight, but the Apaches will have to rely on their ears mostly."

Al jammed a carbine into the saddle scabbard. "She's all loaded, Mitch," he said. He knew that Apaches had very good ears indeed. "You make 'em pay if they find you."

"They won't find me."

"Good luck, Mitch," Falwell said.

"Good luck," Peggy and Winslow echoed.

McHenry gave Mitch a light thump on the leg. "You get yourself back to Sarah and the kids even if you can't help us."

"I'll get us all back, Jason." Mitch touched the brim of his hat in a brief salute. "See you, folks." He gave the horse a kick and the animal headed off.

Nobody else moved. They all watched Mitch quickly disappear into the darkness. Only the slight click of a horseshoe on a stone told them that Mitch was still moving.

Peggy asked McHenry, "Does Mitch have a family?"

"Yeah, six kids. Or actually nine. Three of them, along with his first wife, Katy, were killed by Apaches. Those two Harrington boys taken by the Apaches reminded him too much of his own lost kids. I could see it eating at him."

"That's so sad," she said in anguish.

"It's a hard country." McHenry clenched his teeth as he thought of his dead brother, who had died naturally from illness. "Mighty hard."

Peggy sighed. "It is as you say, Mr. McHenry."

"Yeah." McHenry shifted his Winchester to the other hand. "But let's get going." He turned to the others. "I think the best way is for me to head out by myself and have the rest of you follow. With Falwell's bad leg and Miss Winslow along, you won't be able to move very fast. If I meet up with trouble, I'll make plenty of noise, and that'll give you people a chance to get ready for it."

"Makes sense to me," Al said.

Falwell nodded. "Yes, to me too. I'm sorry about my leg, but I just can't move fast."

"I'll leave the best trail I can," McHenry told them.

The party gathered together what little they could. They had no food or water. However, with the weapons captured from the bandits, each man was able to carry a carbine and a pistol, and they also scavenged all the ammunition they could. McHenry and Al each had a bandolier across his shoulder. The other men stuffed cartridges into their pockets.

"Give me a ten-minute head start," McHenry said. "If I hear somebody coming up behind me, I want to be able to assume it's a bandit."

"Understood," Falwell said. "Good luck."

"Yeah." McHenry sighed. "Good luck to all of us."

As McHenry started out, he waved a good-bye toward Billy's grave behind the station. They had dug the grave hurriedly but deeply, and Al had fashioned a crude cross to put at the head. Al had even managed a few words after the burial, but mostly they had all just stood there in silence for a minute.

They hadn't bothered to bury the dead bandits.

McHenry held the Winchester in both hands as he walked. He didn't walk fast, because he didn't want to blunder into the bandits or make a lot of noise. Also, he didn't want to wander off the trail of the stagecoach.

Following the stagecoach's trail did not turn out to be too difficult. Even though the dim moonlight was not very helpful, the desert soil had given easily under the weight of the stagecoach. The vehicle had left grooves, and McHenry could feel the ridges with his feet much of the time. When he lost the grooves with his feet, he could find the trail again by crouching down and scanning the dirt.

He stopped every minute to listen and to search the surrounding low black hills for any sight or sound that would give away the presence of another human. All he could see, however, were a few silhouettes of hills and low sagebrush, and all he could hear was a slight whisper of breeze in the sagebrush and an occasional nighthawk as it flew about and hunted for insects.

McHenry had no watch, but he estimated that he must have been on the trail almost two hours when the land turned rocky. He got worried, because the stage no longer left grooves all the time. He could only keep on in the direction the stage had last been going when the grooves disappeared and hope it hadn't turned.

He noticed that he was approaching the high cliffs of the canyon lands he had seen from the stage station earlier in the day. The stage had been heading steadily straight for the cliffs, where the bandits would like the hiding places afforded by the canyons.

Then he found the stagecoach. It was lying on its side on a slope. A dead horse lay twisted in its harness. The other five horses were gone.

McHenry approached slowly, even though he was pretty sure no one was there. He made a wide circle of the stage, trying to see anything in the darkness. Finally he went closer.

The bandits had ransacked the contents of the stage-coach. He wasn't surprised that his gold pieces were gone, but the bandits had also taken his extra clothes, his blanket, shaving kit, and even the picture of his parents. Now all he had to show for all his hard work over the years was what he was wearing or carrying. It was now even worse than Mitch had said earlier on the stagecoach.

McHenry climbed up on the stagecoach and looked inside the door of the vehicle. He was surprised not to see Totten. He got back off and searched around the stage. Still no Totten.

He started toward the canyons. Occasionally the rocky ground was broken by stretches of sand. He could see the prints left by horses. When he looked back, though, he found it hard in the darkness to sort out his own tracks from those of the horses. What would the others do? Follow the horses as he was doing? He decided to go back to the stagecoach and wait.

He waited a long time, long enough to get worried again. He figured that it must have been over an hour before he heard the shuffling and crunching that announced someone was coming. Finally he could see figures approaching.

"Al?" McHenry barked.

Silence fell. He heard a pistol being cocked.

"That you, McHenry?" Al called.

"Yeah, it's me. Come on forward."

Al and Falwell came up to McHenry, but Peggy simply sat down where she stopped. Her father stayed with her.

"How are you doing?" McHenry asked Al and Falwell.

"My leg's killing me," Falwell said, "but I'll manage. It's Miss Winslow I'm concerned about."

Winslow growled, "It's hard to walk on this ground." He fussed over his daughter for a moment and then joined the other men. "She's not used to this kind of effort." He wiped his brow. He had worked up a sweat even in the cool of the desert night. "And for that matter, neither am I. I'm exhausted."

"Anything left?" Al waved a hand toward the wreckage of the stagecoach.

"Nothing that we can use," McHenry said. "They were thorough, real good scavengers."

"I don't suppose my valise is still there," Winslow said.

"Yes, but it's empty. Cleaned me out good too."
Winslow sighed.

"Leave any provisions?" Falwell asked hopefully.

"Not a scrap of food and no water. I checked. And they took Totten with them."

"Well, now what?" Winslow asked.

"We go on," McHenry said. "The trail leads into those canyons."

"We can't keep up with you," Falwell said. "And your tracks are getting hard to follow. I don't want to lose you. I think we'd better go on together from here."

"Couldn't we rest here for a little while?" Winslow asked. "My daughter's really tired. And hungry and thirsty too."

"Okay, one minute," McHenry said. "We have to

find those bandits while it's still dark. It must be after midnight already.''

''Mr. McHenry is right,'' Falwell said. ''We will have little chance against them in the daylight.''

''But we may not find them, anyway,'' Winslow protested.

''We have to try,'' McHenry said.

Winslow sighed and plopped to the ground where he was. ''All right. A minute, then.''

McHenry walked over to where Peggy was sitting on the ground. ''How are you doing, Miss Winslow?'' He squatted next to her, resting his Winchester in his lap.

''I can't remember working so hard in my life, and all I'm doing is walking.''

He laughed and smiled. ''At least, you still seem to have a sense of humor.''

She took a deep breath. ''I don't know how anybody survives out here without one. How about you, Mr. McHenry? Do you have a sense of humor?''

''Nothing funny out here, Miss Winslow.'' He had stopped smiling.

''You just smiled. I saw you.''

''Well, I guess I did,'' McHenry admitted. ''But I was smiling more at you than at what you said.''

Peggy looked at him, but she didn't say anything.

''Let me help you to your feet,'' he said. ''I'm sorry, but we have to be moving on.'' He helped her up just as Falwell reached them.

"Anything I can do for you, Miss Winslow?" Falwell asked.

"No, I'm fine. Really," Peggy said.

"I admire your daughter's spirit," McHenry told her father. "She doesn't complain."

"She'll do what she has to," Winslow said. "She's that kind of woman." He got to his feet too.

"Lead on, Mr. McHenry." Peggy forced a smile.

"Yes, ma'am." McHenry couldn't suppress another smile. Then he spoke to all of them: "I think Al should bring up the rear this time. You three stick together in the middle. Let's go."

The party started out again. Soon they entered a canyon. It was broad, probably a half mile in width. The floor was rocky but with broad patches of sandy soil and scrubby sagebrush and cacti. McHenry could pick up the hoofprints often enough to be confident he was still on the trail.

He moved even more slowly than he had before, and he looked back frequently to make sure the others were keeping up. He could see that Peggy was keeping up with all of them.

After half an hour Falwell called to him in a loud whisper. "Sh!" McHenry cautioned as he walked back. "What is it?" he whispered.

Falwell pointed back down the trail. "Al's fallen behind. I don't see him anymore."

McHenry looked. There was no one there. But Al

should have been able to keep up with any of them. "How long is it since you've seen him?"

"I last looked back about ten minutes ago. He was there then."

"I don't like it. I'd better go back and look for him. You three stay here. Stay low. Be ready for anything."

McHenry started back the way they had come, moving slowly, scanning both sides of the trail in the darkness. After a couple of minutes, when he heard footsteps coming, he dropped to one knee and raised his Winchester. When he could see the figure coming, he called. "Al?"

"Sh!" Al answered.

McHenry got to his feet and lowered the Winchester. He could see that Al was glancing behind frequently. Al stopped when he reached McHenry.

"Something wrong?" McHenry whispered.

Al nodded. "We're being followed."

Chapter Three

M<small>C HENRY</small> sucked in his breath. "Apaches or bandits?"

"Bandits. Caught a glimpse of one of 'em. And for that matter, they're not sneaking the way Apaches would."

"How many?"

"I think two, but I saw only the one."

McHenry sighed deeply. "Well, we can't get caught in between. We'll have to get rid of the ones following us."

"We could wait right here. The two of us could shoot 'em down easily."

"But only if they just walk right into our ambush. No, just leave me here. I don't want to shoot you by mistake if I have to go hunting for them. You go on and join the others. With surprise, I ought to get both of them by myself. But there may be more around, certainly up ahead. The shooting is going to draw them here. You'll need all the guns we got with the girl and Winslow."

"You got a point," Al said. "But if I hear more than a couple of shots, I'm comin' back to help."

While Al went on ahead, McHenry strode quickly several paces to the side of the trail where there was a clump of sagebrush. The few plants would have been no cover at all in the daylight, but in the dark their branches made pretty good camouflage. He lay down behind the bush.

He drew his pistol and thumbed back the hammer slowly, using both hands on the revolver so there would be no click when the hammer caught on full cock.

Then he waited. Al's crunching footsteps quickly vanished, and there was silence for about ten minutes. Then McHenry heard footsteps coming. A soft grinding in the sand and an occasional slap of shoe leather on a rock.

McHenry raised his pistol tentatively past the edge of the sagebrush, waiting for a target to appear. Finally, in the darkness, he could make out the dim outline of two figures walking in single file carefully along the tracks. The one in front was carrying a rifle at the ready. The one in back was carrying something in one hand, but McHenry couldn't make it out.

McHenry stretched his gun hand forward a bit farther and sighted down the barrel of the pistol. He aimed at the farther figure, and his pistol followed his target as it drew closer. He wanted to be sure of his shots, and needed to get both of them before the man in front leaped away into the darkness.

McHenry was struck by the thought that these two bandits must have been the runts of their respective litters. Although it was dark, he was sure that both these men were quite short. Then he smiled and lowered his pistol.

"Hello, boys," he said.

The two figures jumped. One of them raised his rifle, searching for a target he couldn't see. The other one raised a club.

"Who's there?" the figure with the rifle demanded.

"A friend," McHenry said. "You must be the Harrington boys."

The rifle sagged a little. "That's right," the boy responded. "Are you with the people from the stagecoach?"

"Yes. Lower the rifle, son, so I can get up."

The boy lowered the rifle immediately and started toward McHenry as he stood up. McHenry holstered the pistol and told them his name.

"I'm Austin Harrington," the boy with the rifle said. "This is my kid brother, Jeremy."

"Don't call me a kid," Jeremy protested.

"Shut up!" Austin ordered.

McHenry pointed to the boy's rifle. "That thing loaded?"

"You bet it is. It ain't got the punch of your carbine there, but I can put a bullet through a jackrabbit at a hundred feet, and I figure I could do the same to an Apache or a bandit."

McHenry nodded. "I'll bet you could." He reached slowly for the big stick the other boy was holding. "Looks like you're pretty well armed too, Jeremy."

"I can bust a skull with that," Jeremy said.

"I'll stay out of your way for sure." McHenry handed the stick back to Jeremy. "How old are you, Austin?"

"I'm almost twelve."

"No, you ain't," Jeremy said. "You just turned eleven two months ago."

"You shut up!" Austin scolded. "You ain't even ten yet."

McHenry smiled. "Okay, okay. Let's join up with the other folks."

"Okay," both boys said eagerly.

McHenry started off and the two boys walked alongside him, one on each side. "You must have been watching a long time to know I'm from the stagecoach."

"Yeah," Austin said. "We've been hiding ever since the Apaches showed up."

"They didn't see you?"

"No. Pa made us sneak out the back as soon as he saw 'em comin'."

"Did you see, uh, everything?" McHenry asked.

"Yeah," Austin murmured. "I was gonna help Pa, but he'd told us not to. He said we'd just get killed too if they attacked."

"We figure Pa got six or seven of them Apaches

before they got him," Jeremy said proudly. "He made 'em pay good."

"Sounds like your pa was a tough hombre."

"He was," Austin agreed. "And I'm gonna grow up just like him. And I'm gonna kill me a hundred Apaches before I'll say it's enough."

"I understand how you feel."

Al came rushing forward. Falwell, Winslow, and Peggy were right behind him.

"Here are your bandits," McHenry told Al. "The Harrington boys. This is Austin and Jeremy."

"Hey, we know you," Austin said, pointing to Al. "You drive one of the stages."

"I sure do, boys. Good to see you, real good to see you." He and the others clapped each boy on the back.

"Gotta talk to you," Al told McHenry.

"Just a second, Al."

Peggy spoke tentatively: "Are you boys the sons of the stage-station manager?"

"Yes, ma'am," they both said.

"Why didn't you join us instead of just follow us?"

"Well," Austin explained, "we stayed hiding while those outlaws were around. We were gonna join you after dark, but you took off and we couldn't catch up right away. I figured you were following the stagecoach that ran away, but then I couldn't figure out why you kept on goin'. So then I didn't want to catch up to you until I could figure out what you were doin'. Gotta watch out for my brother and me both, you see."

"I can watch out for myself!" Jeremy protested.

"I'm the oldest, and I watch out for you. That's the way it is, and don't give no sass."

"McHenry," Al said, "this is important."

"Wait, wait, Al."

Peggy stretched a hand to a shoulder of each boy. "You boys know that your father is—"

"Dead," Austin said. "Apaches killed him. We know that, ma'am."

"You saw it?" she asked, her voice trembling.

"Yes, ma'am."

Peggy wiped tears from her eyes, and then drew the boys to her. Both boys giggled. "I think all three of us should have a good cry," she said.

The boys drew away, reluctantly.

"Naw," Austin said. "Pa wouldn't like that. Men don't cry. Ain't that right, Mr. McHenry?"

"They don't seem to," he agreed.

"Well, I think that's stupid," Peggy said. "Somebody needs to do some crying around here. This country is too hard . . . just too hard. I don't blame you for wanting to move to Chicago, Mr. McHenry."

"Chicago?" Austin repeated. "Why would you want to leave here?"

McHenry just looked at the boy.

"Say," Jeremy said, "you got any food or water?"

"Afraid not, son," McHenry replied. "That's what we're trying to find. We're after those bandits that showed up at the station."

"Oh, so that's it. Say, you sure handled them good back at the station. I can help you now. I can shoot, like I said."

"McHenry!" Al snapped.

"What? What?" McHenry said.

"Come here." Al motioned with his hand, then stalked off to the side a short distance.

McHenry joined him. "What's the problem?"

"The problem is that I don't think either of those boys could have been the bandit I saw."

"You sure?" McHenry looked into the darkness and brought up his Winchester. He realized that he hadn't been paying any attention to possible danger.

"This older boy ain't anywhere near as tall as the fellow I saw."

"It was dark. Maybe—"

Al shook his head. "And I could swear he was wearing a big sombrero. Not an ordinary hat like these boys are wearing."

McHenry stared out into the darkness. He took a deep breath and let it out slowly. "I'll just have to go back."

"We should go together," Al said.

"We're likely to shoot each other."

"But it just don't seem right your goin' alone."

"I could miss them in the dark," McHenry said. "And then they'll land right on top of you. You're needed here. In fact, I think it'd be a good idea if you moved everyone off the trail and took cover with the cliffs at your backs.''

''Okay, but I don't know if I can stay sittin' still once the shootin' starts.''

As McHenry started back down the tracks, the stage driver headed for the rest of the group. McHenry didn't walk directly on the tracks, because the bandits would be coming up them. Instead, he walked off to the side. Sometimes he had to go back to the tracks to make sure he was still moving parallel to them. He frequently stopped and listened and scrutinized the darkness. He saw nothing moving. He was beginning to think that maybe Al had imagined the bandit with the sombrero.

And then he heard laughter.

He dropped to one knee and brought the Winchester to bear in the direction of the voices. They were speaking Spanish. Al had been right.

But the voices and the laughter were way off to the side, not down the trail. Puzzled, McHenry lowered the Winchester. Would the bandits be making that much noise if they were trailing his party?

He got to his feet and slowly headed for the sound of the men. Finally he caught a shadowy glimpse of them. He could make out two men, walking not up the trail but away from it. In fact, they were headed straight for the canyon wall in the opposite direction. They talked occasionally, apparently joking, and didn't seem to be in a hurry.

He followed at a distance, keeping the trail more by

the sound of the two men in front of him than by being able to see them. They reached the canyon wall.

And then they disappeared. McHenry stopped. He couldn't hear them anymore, and the canyon wall was simply a curtain of blackness. He didn't think that they had suddenly tried to hide. They hadn't acted as if they knew they were being followed. The only thing that made sense to him was that the bandits had known about a pass or a trail out of the canyon, perhaps to a neighboring canyon. And the only reason they would have for taking a pass here would be to take a shortcut back to their camp, a shortcut that couldn't be managed by horses. That's why the two bandits had been in the canyon on foot. If he could follow the two bandits, he could find their camp.

Cautiously he moved forward again and reached the canyon wall. But at this point it was a jumble of rocks piled up at the foot of the sheer cliff. He must have missed the spot where the bandits reached the canyon wall.

He had to find the trail again, but was it to the left or right? He thought it was probably to the left, and he hurried that way, quickening his pace. Perhaps he could pick up the sound of their voices or laughter if he were right at the entrance of the canyon pass.

McHenry froze. The hairs on his neck stood up. The sixth sense that a man develops out in this country suddenly told him that he was no longer alone. Had he heard a breath? Smelled body odor? Heard a foot move?

A swish of cloth close to his right side made him whirl about and bring the Winchester up, but a body slammed into his and knocked him down. He pushed the attacker off, but the man scampered to his feet, and he saw dim moonlight glint off the knife blade in the man's right hand. As the hand came down, McHenry smashed it with the carbine and the knife went spinning.

A hand grabbed the barrel of his Winchester. The attacker was strong. The two men wrestled over the carbine, and the other man smashed a fist into McHenry's face. McHenry grunted but didn't let go of the carbine. He tripped the man with a foot and they both went down.

They rolled on the ground, legs flailing, each man with both hands on the carbine and trying to jerk it away from the other. They rolled over and over. On the last roll McHenry felt the impression of the knife under his back.

McHenry let go of the carbine and the other man rolled free. But McHenry had the knife in his hand before the other man, still on the ground, swiveled the carbine toward him. McHenry swung his arm in a wide arc, and the knife plunged deep into the man's chest.

The man screamed, and the Winchester exploded with a crash and a flash of light. The shot went wild. The attacker slumped on the ground.

McHenry's hand was still on the knife handle. He was panting fiercely from the struggle and the fright, and only slowly did he let go of the knife. He flopped over on his back and tried to catch his breath. Then he sat up slowly. He picked up the Winchester and carefully levered another cartridge into the chamber.

Then he heard footsteps running his way, but not from the canyon pass. He jumped to his feet and stepped off to the side. He saw the man. He wore no sombrero.

"Al?" he called.

Al slid to a stop. "You all right?"

"Yeah, for now."

Al rushed up. "I couldn't wait. You took so long, I started to follow you. Then I heard the scuffle and I came running. When I heard that shot, I thought I was too late." He looked over at the body. "You got one of them, but that shot may rouse the rest. It was really loud in this night air."

"The problem's worse than that," McHenry said. "Take a close look at that fellow."

"Huh?" Al stepped over to the body, looked down, and muttered, "An Apache."

Chapter Four

"McHenry," Al said, "Apaches are like cockroaches. You never find just *one* of 'em."

McHenry wiped a hand over his mouth. His hand was still shaking. "I was hoping they'd left for Mexico by now."

"Seems they think there's still good pickings here for a while."

"Wonder if they know about Peggy Winslow," McHenry said.

"We can't be sure, but I'll bet they do. Since this is an Apache, what happened to the bandits I saw?"

McHenry pointed to the canyon wall. "You were right. There were two bandits, but they weren't following us. My guess is, they went back to the stagecoach to plunder some more."

"Why did they go on foot?"

"There must be a pass through or over this canyon wall that a horse couldn't handle," McHenry said. "But it was so much quicker to get back to the stage that way that the bandits decided to go afoot."

"Then we must be pretty close to their camp." Al looked at the cliff. "Do you know where the trail is?"

"I think it's not far off to the left somewhere."

"Should we go back and get the others?"

McHenry shook his head. "I don't think we have time. Like you said, that shot may have alerted them already, even the two guys I was following."

"Maybe we were lucky. These canyons can do funny things to sounds. You might hear a gunshot miles down the canyon, but not up on top of it. Maybe just the two of us should follow them."

"Okay," McHenry said. "Let's try to find that trail."

They walked close to the cliff face, always searching for a small defile that would reveal a trail to the top. And they found it shortly. It was a narrow opening where vertical layers of rock had separated. No horse could have fit through the defile, and even a man had to step sideways sometimes. The sand and dust on the bottom of the defile showed unmistakable bootprints when McHenry got down on his hands and knees to look.

"Up we go," he said. "Single file."

The trail was flat for a short distance, but it soon rose steeply, and finally it consisted of a series of ledges and outcroppings that served as steps.

The trail reached only halfway to the top of the canyon wall. It started downhill again for a short distance and then leveled off, still far above the canyon floor. In a quarter of an hour the trail opened, and McHenry and Al found themselves entering another canyon. They could clearly hear voices ahead.

"Is that a light I see over there?" Al asked.

McHenry nodded. "Must be reflections from a campfire. Be real quiet. Watch the rocks for a sentry."

They advanced slowly, searching for each step carefully. They held their Winchesters ready.

They met no sentry, and simply came upon the campsite. It was well below them, though. They stopped immediately and backed up before they were seen. They crouched down, crept over to some large rocks, and peered down at the camp.

Even in the relatively dim light of the bandits' campfire, they could see that they were in a much narrower canyon than the previous one. And there were trees in this one, short stunted cottonwoods and what looked like mesquite farther down the canyon. Those trees had provided sufficient firewood.

The campfire was burning in the center of the camp, and a big iron pot hung from a tripod over the fire. The fire was still big enough that flames licked around the pot. None of the bandits were eating, however. They were lounging about the camp and talking.

McHenry tapped Al. "Their horses are over there." There was a picket line, almost invisible in the darkness, in a small grove of scrubby trees.

"More horses than there are bandits. I count ten men, and not a one of 'em is asleep. This isn't going to be easy. How come they're all still awake at this hour?''

''Maybe they can't sleep after what we did to them earlier. Anyway, I think there's nine,'' McHenry said. ''If I'm not mistaken, that's Totten sitting there with his back to us.''

Suddenly, the bandit leader yanked the sitting man to his feet and shoved him roughly toward the fire.

''Yup,'' Al said. ''That's Totten all right.''

''Wonder what that guy's got in mind?''

As the bandit leader picked up a long whip, Totten put up his hands and started begging. The leader laughed, lashed out with the whip, and slashed Totten across the back. Then Totten started to dance.

All the bandits laughed. Some cheered and raised bottles or clapped. The leader cracked the whip over Totten's head and he danced faster.

''Like a cat with a mouse,'' McHenry said.

''Mouse is right.'' Al sighed. ''What do you want to do? The odds are pretty uneven.''

''I know. I was hoping there wouldn't be any more of them than we saw at the station. Now I wish that Falwell was here.''

''Yeah. Or even that kid.''

McHenry smiled weakly, but the smile faded quickly. ''There can't be much darkness left. If we went back now to get Falwell, it would be light before we returned.''

''We can't get much closer from here.''

McHenry considered for a moment, and then said, "I'm going to sneak over by the horses. Looks like there's plenty of rocks there. I can keep them from the horses, and when I open up on them, you join in. Let's hope the surprise will drive them over to the other side of the canyon. Then you head for the horses too, and we'll set them loose and hightail it out of here. With all of us on horses and the bandits afoot, we won't have to worry about them anymore."

"Okay. What about Totten?" Al asked.

"I don't think there's anything we can do for him, Al. Do you? There's only two of us."

"They'll probably shoot him as soon as we open up."

"We need the horses," McHenry pointed out. "Think about the others waiting for us."

Al sighed. "You're right. It's a tough break for him, but we gotta think of everyone."

"And maybe his luck will hold. I'm surprised he's not already dead. Okay, I'm heading over toward the horses, and you be ready to shoot as soon as I do. I'll aim for the bandits on the far side and you shoot at the ones over here. No sense our both trying to kill the same ones."

McHenry crouched low. There would be a very short time during which he would be exposed to view from camp, but he counted on the bandits' not paying any attention to the rocks on the hillsides around the camp. They wouldn't be expecting anyone.

"Here I go," he said, and keeping low, he left the shelter of the rocks and headed across the trail. He hadn't covered ten feet before he heard Totten shout: "McHenry! Save me!"

McHenry froze and glared down at the camp. "You fool!" he cried through clenched teeth.

The bandits leaped to their feet. Guns popped into their hands. McHenry raised his Winchester and fired. A bandit pitched backward. McHenry leaped for the rocks on the other side of the trail. Then he and Al poured a rapid fire into the campsite. The bandits were caught in the open in the light from the campfire, and some of them were apparently drunk. Two more of them toppled over from the impact of the slugs from the Winchesters. Totten spun around and crashed to the ground. He lay still.

The remaining bandits took cover. Some ducked behind rocks and some scampered in the other direction to disappear into the darkness. The flashes from their guns gave away their positions.

McHenry and Al had their bandoliers full of cartridges, and they poured a heavy fire down into the camp, firing and levering new cartridges into their Winchesters as fast as they could.

One bandit yelped and another simply slumped motionless where he lay on the ground behind a rock without enough protection.

McHenry ducked over to another group of rocks, and from there he concentrated on the bandits firing from the dark on the other side of the camp. He picked one flash of light and studied the bandit's rhythm of firing. He waited, then fired four quick shots. A pistol clattered on the rocks, and McHenry heard a body falling and then sliding down a slope. The bandit leader yelled to his men, and four jumped up and ran for the grove of trees.

McHenry called out to Al, "They're going for the horses! Come on!" He jumped up from behind the rocks and started running for the horse picket line. He slid to a stop halfway down the hill and fired several more shots at the running figures. One of them spun around and crumpled to the ground. McHenry resumed running.

The outlaws reached the horses and furiously un-hitched every one. Those they didn't ride they drove off.

Al and McHenry stopped and fired their Winchesters, and when those were empty, they fired their pistols. Racing away on the horses, the retreating bandits fired back blindly at the two men.

McHenry still had two shots to go when he heard the sickening thwack of lead hitting bone. As his last bullet went after the bandits, he heard Al fall down.

The bandits disappeared into the night. McHenry spun around and saw Al on the ground. He had simply fallen straight backward. His Winchester and pistol lay on the ground next to him, his arms lay almost casually at his side, his overturned hat was crumpled under his head.

McHenry took two quick steps to reach Al's side. He knelt down. The dim moonlight was all that he needed to see the bloody hole in Al's forehead. McHenry groaned.

"It was just a lucky shot, Al," he said, shaking his head.

Cautiously, McHenry made his way down to the camp. There he checked the bodies of the bandits to make sure they were dead, because he didn't want a bullet in his back. He bent over Totten's body and was astonished when Totten rolled over and sat up on one elbow.

"You're still alive!"

"Very much so," Totten said. "Can I get up now?"

McHenry didn't answer, but Totten got to his feet anyway and brushed off his clothes. "And glad to be alive, Mr. McHenry. I owe you my life."

"But Al lost his," McHenry said angrily. "If you'd kept your mouth shut, he'd still be alive."

"You don't know that. With all the bullets flying, he might have been killed anyway. But I'm sorry he was killed."

"By shouting at me, you stopped me from getting to the horses before the bandits. The horses were what we needed the most."

"Well, I'm sorry," Totten said. "How was I to know what you were up to?"

McHenry turned away in disgust and went to the campfire. Gingerly he lifted the cover of the iron pot. The pot was still one-third full of beans. He set the cover down and scooped up some fingers full of beans. They were delicious. "They have any other food around here?" he asked.

"There was some beef jerky somewhere," Totten said. "Maybe some stale bread too."

"Find it," McHenry ordered. "We're going to take these beans back to the others and bring along any other food we can."

McHenry swallowed more beans and savored the flavor. It had been a long time since he'd eaten. He licked his fingers clean and wiped them on his trousers.

He then went through the belongings of each of the bandits. He wasn't interested in more guns—he already had more than he could carry. And he wasn't interested in plunder, his concern now being simple survival. He did take the ammunition that he found, including a second bandolier for himself.

And he stumbled across his money pouch and discovered that the gold coins were still inside. "Well, I'll be!" he said, and he stuck the pouch in his back pocket. It didn't make much of a bulge, because he didn't have many coins. He searched carefully through the booty, but couldn't find any more things that belonged to him. He was sorry most of all about the photograph. But he did find what he had hoped most to find—water.

He opened the first canteen and poured the welcome liquid into his mouth, letting it splash over his chin and dribble down to his shirt.

He found five canteens, and they were all full. He asked Totten, "Is there a spring nearby?"

"On the other side of those trees."

It didn't seem a likely spot for an actual spring, and was probably a deep pool left in the rocks by the spring rains and protected from the sun by constant shade. The Apaches knew about all those kinds of spots, and these bandits probably did too.

Totten nodded down at what he was holding. "Here's all the beef jerky I could find, and one hard loaf of bread, and two more bags of beans."

"Good. The beans will be useful even if they're not cooked." McHenry grabbed the handle of the iron pot and hoisted it off the tripod. "Put all that food in one of the saddlebags over there. Then throw the bag over your shoulder." He handed Totten the pot. "You can carry this too."

"How come I have to carry everything?" Totten complained. He gingerly shifted the hot handle of the iron pot from one hand to the other. "Ouch!"

"Al would have wanted it that way," McHenry said, then proceeded to drape all the canteens over Totten's shoulders too.

Totten grumbled some more, but he settled the saddlebag and canteens as comfortably as he could and then picked up the iron pot. "Satisfied?" he asked sarcastically.

"You'll do," McHenry said. "This way." He headed back up the shortcut trail.

"Are you going to do anything about the stage driver?" Totten asked. "I mean, shouldn't we bury him?"

"I'd make you bury him by yourself if we had time, but we don't. Al would understand."

It took them a long time to get back to the others. By that time visibility had increased tremendously in the early dawn light.

Winslow said to Totten, "We thought you'd been killed."

"No, still very much alive, thank you." Totten set the pot down. "Mr. McHenry rescued me."

"Where's Al?" Falwell asked.

"He's dead," McHenry said. "Bandit bullet."

"Oh, no!" Peggy cried. "He was such a nice man."

"We heard no shooting," Winslow said.

"Most of it was in a neighboring canyon," McHenry told him. "Sound just didn't carry over here." He started taking the canteens from Totten. "Here's water, courtesy of the bandits."

McHenry passed around the canteens, and they drank eagerly.

"What's in the pot?" Falwell asked.

"Beans," McHenry said as he handed the saddlebag

to Winslow. "And there's beef jerky, bread, and raw beans in here."

The group sat down in a big circle for their breakfast. They ate all the cooked beans, using their cupped hands as utensils. The loaf of bread didn't stretch very far with so many people, but even the crumbs tasted good to them. As they washed it all down with another round of drinks from the canteens, they watched the sunlight creep down the opposite canyon walls.

"Easy with the water, folks," McHenry ordered. "That may have to last us for several days." He leaned back against a large rock.

"What happened out there?" Falwell asked.

"First I had a run-in with an Apache," McHenry said. "I had to kill him."

"How did you do it?" Peggy asked.

McHenry looked at her strangely. "We fought. I used his knife."

"How did it feel? How do you feel now?"

"Why the inquisition?" her father asked. "Do you think he did something wrong?"

"No. There just seems to be so much death around here. First back at the stage station. Then here." She flopped her hands wearily in her lap. "I don't know what I mean."

"I did what I had to do, Miss Winslow," McHenry said.

"I understand," she murmured. "Really I do."

"What about the bandits?" Winslow asked. "How did you rescue Totten?"

"Al and I attacked their camp. But Al took a bullet in the head, because—"

"Wait a minute." Totten interrupted. "Don't go blaming me for Al's getting killed."

"Totten—"

Falwell interrupted now. "That's not important right now, is it, McHenry?"

"Not important?" McHenry repeated in disbelief.

"Since you didn't bring back any horses, I assume the bandits got away."

McHenry looked from Falwell to Totten and then back to Falwell. The lieutenant was right. First things first. "Three of them," McHenry said. "We got six before the rest escaped on their horses. They ran off all the other horses too."

"How many of those six did you kill?" Peggy asked.

McHenry looked at her again. Her appearance had changed since the day before. No longer a clean and prim young lady, she was disheveled and dirty and looked exhausted. Her dress was dirty and her hat was gone. She still looked proud and pretty, though. And he didn't care for the way her eyes looked at him so questioningly.

"Probably half of them," McHenry said. "Three of the bandits."

"You say that so matter-of-factly. You just killed

four men. And a total of eight men have died in the last few hours. Is it eight? Or six? Or ten?''

''What's your point, my dear?'' Winslow asked carefully. He sounded worried. ''I don't think you're being fair to Mr. McHenry. In fact, I suggest you just keep quiet about any misgivings you have about what's going on. We are not in a position to be judging—''

''I wasn't judging anyone!'' Peggy snapped. ''It's just that men are human beings, and a lot of men have just died violently. It seems that there should be something more than just counting bodies.''

No one said anything for a while. Then Jeremy spoke. ''Aw, Miss Winslow, they were just bandits and an Apache.''

''They're still men. And the stage driver was no bandit and no Apache, and he's dead too,'' Peggy said. ''By a bullet. Mr. McHenry, did you give him a Christian burial like he gave Billy?''

''I didn't have time, Miss Winslow. I wasn't about to dig a grave when the rest of the bandits could come back at any time.'' Her attitude irritated him, but at the same time he admired her spirit and conviction.

Falwell raised a hand for attention. ''McHenry, do you think the bandits will come after us again?''

McHenry shrugged. ''I suppose they're pretty mad, but I doubt they care much about the members we killed. It all depends on whether they want to chance taking us on now for something they want. The odds are no longer in their favor. They'd have to want it awfully bad.''

''I'll bet they want you,'' Jeremy said to Peggy.

''Shut up!'' Austin growled at his brother.

Peggy folded her hands in her lap. ''It's all right, Austin. I'm realistic about the situation.''

''Well, now what?'' Winslow asked. ''We've got some food and water but no horses. Do we sit here until help comes? Will anybody find us here?''

''Do you suppose anybody's looking for us?'' Peggy peered into the distance.

''What you really mean is, did Mitch get through?'' McHenry said.

''What if he didn't make it? And who would think to look for us where we are now unless Mitch had been there to tell them to look here?''

''They'll look for the stagecoach,'' McHenry explained to her. ''And then they could follow our tracks. Even if Mitch didn't get through, the stage company or the sheriff will surely send someone.''

''Maybe,'' Totten said. ''And maybe not.''

''I'm not saying we should stay right here,'' McHenry told him. ''There was water back in the other canyon by the bandit camp. We could stop there and refill our canteens.''

''On our way to where?'' Winslow asked.

''We can't go far without horses,'' Falwell observed.

''I know.'' McHenry sighed. ''But Miss Winslow

may be right. We are off the beaten path now, and it would be easier for someone to find us if we were back near the stage station. We can't travel far, yet we don't want to be caught in the ruins of the station if the Apaches attack us.''

Austin jumped to his feet. ''We know some good hiding places near the station.''

''Yeah,'' Jeremy joined in. ''You can see the station, but they can't see you.''

''Sounds like the place to go,'' McHenry said. ''So we'll stop back at the bandit camp and refill the canteens on the way.'' He looked up and observed that the sun was halfway across the canyon floor. ''Perhaps we should wait until tonight. It's going to get hot real fast, and traveling at night would be more comfortable. It'll just take us the one evening to make it.''

''Might give the Apaches time to wander off too,'' Falwell said.

McHenry nodded. ''I don't think Apaches ever just wander anywhere. Still, they must be getting uneasy about staying in the area of their last raid for so long. They probably know about that Army patrol Mitch is after. Whether they stop Mitch or not, they just might take off. They want to raid settlements, not fight cavalry.''

''But what about those outlaws that got away?'' Totten asked.

Totten's question was answered by a rifle slug that smashed into the rock McHenry was leaning against. It came close enough to his ear to sting his face with rock fragments.

Chapter Five

PEGGY screamed and McHenry shouted, "Take cover!" Everyone flattened out. McHenry grabbed his Winchester and threw himself behind a rock.

Winslow hustled Peggy over to another rock and Jeremy crowded in next to her. Falwell got behind the same rock as McHenry and brought up his Winchester. Totten crawled between a rock and the cliff face. Austin also found a rock, and he raised his low-caliber rifle and peered over it.

"Do you see 'em?" Austin asked McHenry.

"That shot hit next to my right ear," McHenry said. "It must have come from the right. Must be the bandits."

Sure enough, their leader called out from the rocks: "Hey, señor."

"Find out what he wants," Totten told McHenry.

"I already know what he wants," McHenry said. "You don't make deals with someone like that."

"Señor," the bandit leader called again, "you kill a lot of my men."

"As if you care," McHenry shouted back.

"I no want to fight anymore, señor. I want to go home."

McHenry peered over the rock. "Then go home. We're not stopping you." He ducked back down and tapped Falwell. "I saw one of them. He's over on the right about a third of the way up the cliff, on a ledge. He was watching us, not staying out of sight. If I keep this guy talking, maybe we can spot all of them."

Falwell nodded vigorously. "If we know where they are, we have a better chance against them."

"What do you want from us, mister?" McHenry called.

"You have something we want, señor. The woman."

McHenry glanced over at Peggy. She showed no response, but Winslow gritted his teeth and clenched his carbine tighter.

"You just expect us to hand her over to you?" McHenry called.

"No, we make a deal."

Falwell ducked down. "There's another one almost straight in front of us. He's lying behind a sagebrush bush."

McHenry nodded. "Good. But I still didn't see the guy I'm talking to."

"I see him," Austin said. "He's in the rocks at the foot of the cliff on the right."

McHenry called to the leader again: "What kind of deal you got in mind?"

Winslow snarled, "McHenry, I'll kill you if you try to—"

McHenry waved him silent. "Don't worry."

"There are Apaches here, señor," the bandit called.

"So?"

"You need horses, no? I trade you horses for the woman."

McHenry looked over at Winslow and Peggy. Jeremy clung to her tighter. Winslow was fuming. Peggy looked ashamed and humiliated.

"How many?" McHenry called.

"Six, señor. One for each man and boy to ride away. Be safe from Apache."

"Let me think a minute, mister."

Winslow snarled at McHenry, "Six horses for my daughter! That's barbaric!"

McHenry raised a hand. "Easy, easy, Winslow. I wouldn't trade your daughter away for anything. Let's get ready, fellas. I can see all three bandits now. They've got their heads up watching us, and that one on the cliff is kneeling in plain sight."

"You want to try now?" Falwell asked.

"Falwell, you take the one in front of us. He's a smaller target. I'll take the one on the cliff." He looked back for Totten, but the man was out of sight behind the rock. "Totten!"

"I'm scared," Totten said. "Just shoot them."

McHenry was disgusted. "All right, Winslow and Austin, you two shoot at the leader in the rocks over at the right."

"I'm not sure I can hit him," Winslow said, "but I'm sure going to try. He insulted my daughter."

"I think *I* can hit him," Austin said.

McHenry nodded. "Try. Falwell and I will join you. Everybody ready?" Everyone nodded. "Okay. Then wait for my word." He stuck his head above the rock and called, "You got a deal!"

"*Bueno!*" the bandit cried.

"Now!" McHenry said.

McHenry, Falwell, and Winslow brought up their Winchesters and Austin his rifle. The guns roared.

McHenry's first bullet caught his target in the shoulder. The man yelped and jumped back from his kneeling position. His second bullet smacked into the rocks and the bandit tried to retreat. But the third bullet bounced him off the rock face and he tumbled off the ledge.

Falwell fired only two bullets. The first bullet kicked sand in the outlaw's face and the second one snuffed out his life. He then turned his attention to the bandit leader.

Winslow and Austin were shooting. Winslow didn't really know where the bandit was but he fired anyhow. Suddenly he cried out and spun around and slid to the ground. He dropped his carbine and grimaced and clapped a hand on his shoulder.

"Father!" Peggy screamed. She jumped up and rushed to his side. "You're hurt!" She tried to lift his hand from the wound in his shoulder. Blood was seeping between his fingers.

Winslow spoke through clenched teeth: "I didn't even see him until he shot me."

"I winged him!" Austin shouted.

McHenry and Falwell both fired once in the direction of the bandit. "You're right, Austin," McHenry said. "Good shooting." He looked toward Peggy and her father. "Are you hit bad, Winslow?" he called.

Winslow shook his head. "I'll be okay. Just not used to this, McHenry." Peggy was stuffing a handkerchief into the wound.

McHenry jumped to his feet and told Falwell, "I'm going after him."

"I'm coming with you." Falwell got to his feet too, though much slower than McHenry. They started forward, dodging from rock to rock. "Cover us," McHenry called back.

"Don't worry," Austin yelled.

McHenry and Falwell were halfway to the bandit's last position when the man jumped from behind a rock and started running in the opposite direction. Falwell and McHenry stopped and fired their Winchesters. The bandit went down.

When McHenry and Falwell reached the man, he was furiously trying to crawl behind a rock. Blood flowed from a leg wound, and there was another wound in his side. Awkwardly he tried to raise a pistol.

McHenry was upon the bandit before he could bring the pistol to bear. McHenry batted it out of the outlaw's hand with the butt of his carbine. The bandit slumped down, panting heavily.

"Ah, señor, you tricked me," he said.

"Isn't that what you intended to do to us? You should have kept riding."

"Now the Apaches will get all of you."

McHenry shook his head. "We've got your horses now."

"You have to find them first."

"They can't be too far away," Falwell said.

"But we're in a hurry, mister." McHenry drew his pistol and cocked it. He pointed it at the outlaw's head. "Perhaps this will loosen your tongue. Where are the horses?"

The outlaw laughed. "You will kill me anyway, señor. So shoot. Then the Apaches get you."

McHenry aimed the pistol at the outlaw's good leg. "There are worse things than dying."

The outlaw shook his head. McHenry fired into the ground next to the bandit's leg.

The bandit leader flinched and then relaxed. "Shoot all you want, señor."

"He's not going to tell us," Falwell said. "We'll have to find the horses on our own. And quickly."

"Last chance, mister." McHenry pointed his pistol at the outlaw's head again.

"The Apache will roast you over fire. Both of you. All of you. And the woman?" The bandit smiled happily. "Ah, the pain will be terrible, no?"

"So long, mister," McHenry said. "This is for Al."

"No!" Peggy screamed.

McHenry's head spun round. "Stay back!" he ordered.

"Don't watch this," Falwell told Peggy.

But she came running up. "What are you going to do—shoot the man as he's lying there?" She was out of breath and distraught.

"What do you suggest we do with him?" McHenry asked sarcastically.

"He's a prisoner now. We'll take him with us."

McHenry's pistol hand sagged as he gaped at her in astonishment. "Take him with us? Are you daft? We're worried about our own survival, Miss Winslow. We can't be burdened by a prisoner, and a wounded one at that. He's a murderer, and the law will just hang him if we manage to get him back to town."

She pointed at his pistol. "And that would be murder too."

"I have to side with McHenry," Falwell said. "We can't—"

"You'll be as much a murderer as he if you shoot him like this, Mr. McHenry," Peggy said sternly. "We can take him with us. I'll tend to his wounds."

"He wounded your own father," McHenry reminded her. "He tried to kill him, in fact."

"But now he's defenseless." Peggy took a step closer to him. "Put the gun down, Mr. McHenry. Please."

"How about if we just leave him here," he suggested.

"To bleed to death? Or be killed by the Apaches?"

"Miss Winslow," McHenry said, "this isn't making sense. Taking him with us will jeopardize our own lives."

Peggy reached out and put a hand on his gun arm. "Please," she murmured.

McHenry glanced down at her hand, a fine hand with slim fingers, only slightly tanned. Her touch was exciting.

Next he glanced over at Falwell, but the officer's eyes showed as much confusion as McHenry felt.

Peggy gave McHenry's arm a slight squeeze. "Please, I can't stand all this. Don't shoot him. Take him with us. Hand him over to the law."

McHenry looked into her pleading eyes. Slowly he turned to look down at the bandit leader.

"Well, señor?" the Mexican asked. He smiled, taking pleasure in McHenry's dilemma.

McHenry was sure that the man was resigned to dying. He had led a violent life and expected its end to be the same. This predicament of McHenry's was funny to him. Life had been a cruel joke, anyway.

"Tell you what, Miss Winslow," McHenry said finally. "We'll just leave him right here until we find the horses. If we find the horses and there's enough of them, we'll take him with us. If not, he'll have to stay behind. That's the best I can do."

"All right," she agreed.

"Go get your father and Austin. They'll have to guard him."

As Peggy scampered back toward their little camp, McHenry looked at Falwell and said, "We really should shoot him." He was hoping that Falwell had stronger resolve than he did.

Falwell frowned. "Without a horse, he'd be as good as dead."

"Meaning we should make sure not to find enough horses?"

"Well. . . ."

They looked down at the bandit. He just smiled again, laughed once, and then, breathing heavily, slumped back in exhaustion.

Austin, Winslow, and Peggy came up.

"I'm okay," Winslow said. "It hurts, but the bleeding is pretty well stopped."

"Good," McHenry said. "You two watch this guy. If he tries anything, shoot him." He looked at Peggy sternly. She nodded slightly. He turned to Falwell. "Come on. Let's backtrack these bandits."

The two men set off. The trail was not too difficult to follow. It was bright daylight now, so they made

quick progress, and before long the trail entered a narrow defile of yellow rock with steep walls. The floor
was sand mixed with many fallen rocks.

McHenry and Falwell followed the trail through the
defile. It soon opened up into a shallow basin with no
other outlet that a horse could take. In the basin were
a dozen bandit horses. And with the horses were nearly
two dozen Apache warriors.

Chapter Six

EVERY man in the canyon was surprised by the sudden meeting. Carbines came up and men shot from the hip. Bullets spattered into the canyon walls around McHenry and Falwell, kicking up spouts of yellow dust.

The Apaches headed for the rocks, McHenry and Falwell turned and ran, and the horses bolted and raced after the two white men.

"Look out!" Falwell shouted. He jumped to the side and McHenry did likewise. The horses thundered into the defile.

"Try to grab one!" McHenry shouted.

But the horses were frightened, and two men reaching for them merely heightened their fear. Falwell tripped on his bad leg, fell to his hands and knees, and then jumped up and flattened himself against the canyon wall.

McHenry grabbed a bridle and cried "Whoa, whoa!" but the animal didn't stop. He pulled back as hard as he could, and though the horse's neck was twisted, the mount turned sideways in the canyon and kept pumping his legs. The next horse in line swerved to avoid the first one, and McHenry was trapped between them. The two charging horses squashed him, rolled him between them, and threw him to the ground. He curled up into a ball. The stampede went over him and he was knocked in a spin.

When the last horse sped by, Falwell started firing his Winchester at the Apaches coming into the defile. He reached down to help McHenry, who was slow in rising.

"Are you hurt?" Falwell asked quickly.

McHenry was trying to get his breath back. He slowly uncurled and started to get up. "I got kicked pretty hard," he said, reaching for his Winchester.

Falwell fired again. "Get up quick! Those Apaches will be charging down this canyon next!"

McHenry shook his head to clear it. Falwell gave him a hand, and McHenry got to his feet and scooped up his Winchester.

They both ran. McHenry was slower than Falwell at first, notwithstanding Falwell's bruised leg. But as McHenry's breath came back and his head stopped spinning, he caught up with Falwell. They looked back frequently, but the defile twisted enough so that the pursuing Apaches couldn't get a shot at them.

The two men burst from the canyon and headed to the left, racing along the cliff face. They noticed that the bandits' horses had scattered across the desert.

McHenry and Falwell kept running. Finally, panting

and stumbling, they came to the spot where they had left the bandit leader and his guards. But no one was there.

McHenry and Falwell stopped and tried to catch their breath. McHenry glanced back. ''The Apaches are right on our tail.'' He raised his carbine and fired.

Peggy screamed. McHenry and Falwell spun their heads around. Falwell pointed as he cried, ''They're back in the camp.''

As a shot was fired in the camp, McHenry and Falwell broke into a run again. When they reached the group in the rocks, they slid to a stop. The bandit leader staggered to his feet with an arm around Peggy's throat. He jerked her roughly to her feet. Peggy clutched at the man's arm and gasped for air. He pointed a pistol at McHenry and Falwell.

McHenry saw Winslow lying on the ground, his fingers digging into his belly. Austin was sitting on the ground holding his head. His rifle was nowhere to be seen. Jeremy was huddled against the cliff face. Totten was peering out from behind a rock on the far side of the camp. His hands were pressed on top of the rock, and McHenry could see he had no gun.

''Welcome, amigos,'' the bandit leader said. ''You will drop your guns, please.''

McHenry glanced over his shoulder. The Apaches had disappeared. He looked back at the Mexican and Peggy. ''This is crazy,'' he said. ''There are twenty Apaches heading this way.''

"I know that. But why should I surrender?" he asked. "No, señor, you throw down your guns. I take the woman, then you pick up your guns and fight the Apache. I will be gone."

"How do we know you won't simply shoot us?" Falwell asked.

"I could do that now, señor, but I want you to stop the Apaches for a while. They will kill you, but I will have time to leave."

Winslow groaned. "I'm sorry, McHenry," he said, keeping his eyes tightly closed. "I was distracted by the shooting, and he jumped us. I didn't think he could even move with his wounds."

McHenry didn't say anything. He looked at Peggy. He wondered if she, too, was now thinking that he should have shot the bandit when he had the chance. Certainly the look in her eyes was now one of fear.

The bandit staggered forward a step. He and Peggy slumped against a rock.

McHenry could see that the man was weak and could hardly put any pressure on his wounded leg. The blood had saturated the bandage Peggy had applied.

"Now! Drop your guns now!" The man was sweating profusely.

Falwell acted first. "All right," he said. He dropped his carbine.

The bandit shifted his pistol's aim toward McHenry. "And you, señor?"

McHenry glanced backward slowly. Still no sign of

the Apaches. Maybe they were curious about what was going on here. Certainly they must be watching.

He looked back at the bandit leader. The Mexican blinked his eyes. The sweat was blinding him.

Austin was crawling on his hands and knees behind the bandit toward where Winslow had dropped his pistol.

McHenry watched him. "Okay, mister," he said. Slowly he started to lower his carbine. It plopped onto the ground. "How are you going to move? You can hardly stand. Let the woman go and we won't try to stop you."

"No. She goes with me." He forced himself to stand upright, pulling Peggy with him. He didn't relax his desperate grip. Peggy's face was red.

"Then stay with us," McHenry said. "We'll take care of you. The woman will take care of you. She made us promise we wouldn't hurt you." Austin had reached Winslow's pistol.

The bandit laughed. "I am not stupid. You kill me if I let go of woman."

McHenry silently agreed with the man. Austin picked up the pistol and got to his knees. He held the pistol in both hands and raised it. He used both thumbs to bring the hammer back first to half cock and then full cock.

The bandit stiffened at the double click.

Austin pointed the pistol at the bandit's back. "Hey, mister," he said.

The bandit turned, off balance, bringing his gun hand around. Austin squinted and pulled the trigger.

The bullet plowed into the bandit's side. It broke his grip on Peggy and threw him against a large rock. Peggy dropped to the ground, clutching at her throat. The bandit hissed through clenched teeth. His wavering hand tried to point his pistol at the boy.

Austin was using both hands to get the pistol cocked again, but McHenry drew his own pistol. His first shot made the outlaw stiffen. The second shot knocked him off the rock and sprawled him on the ground.

McHenry and Falwell grabbed their carbines and rushed forward. McHenry dropped to his knees next to Peggy. "Are you hurt?" he asked.

She shook her head slowly. There were tears in her eyes. "I was wrong," she said.

McHenry helped her to her feet and they both hurried over to where Winslow lay on his back, still clutching his belly.

McHenry was nervous, and he quickly scanned the desert and rocks for any sign of Apaches. None were visible, which didn't mean they weren't there.

Austin was still kneeling in the sand and staring at the dead bandit. The boy still held the pistol with both hands, and still pointed it at the outlaw leader.

"You're a good man to have around," McHenry told him.

Austin's frown disappeared. "Thanks," he said.

Falwell joined McHenry, and both men looked down

at Winslow. The bloodstain on his shirt was widening, and they exchanged worried glances.

Peggy had put a hand under her father's head. Her other hand was fussing with the hair on his brow. Tears were rolling down both cheeks. She kept repeating softly, "I'm sorry, I'm sorry."

"My own fault, dear," Winslow whispered. "I should never have taken my eyes off him."

Peggy lifted one of his hands from his wound. She grimaced at the jagged hole in his vest and shirt. "We have to stop the bleeding," she said. She pulled back the skirt of her dress, tugged at the white petticoat beneath, and tore a strip off the bottom. She then lifted Winslow's other hand and unbuttoned his vest and a few of the lower buttons on his shirt. As she stuffed the cloth inside the shirt, Winslow grimaced in pain. Finally she laid both his hands back over the wound, holding the cloth against it.

Winslow looked at McHenry and then Falwell. "This is a bad wound, isn't it?"

"I've seen men survive worse wounds than that," Falwell assured him.

"Me too," McHenry said, but he was lying.

Winslow closed his eyes. "I was in the Fiftieth Pennsylvania back in the War Between the States. A gut shot was almost always fatal."

"Father," Peggy urged, "don't talk like that. You're going to make it. I know it."

McHenry touched Winslow's arm gently. "We'll

get you to a doctor. The war was a long time ago. Doctors are better nowadays.''

Winslow replied with a wry smile, ''How do you propose to get me to a doctor? Will the Apaches carry me?''

McHenry didn't have an answer to that question, and he patted Winslow's arm. ''We'll do it somehow, sir.'' He stood up and crooked a finger at Falwell. Crouching low, he stepped over to a large rock, knelt down behind it, and looked over the rock to scan the desert and the cliffs again.

Falwell joined him behind the rock, saying, ''I still don't see any Apaches.''

''I don't know what they're up to, but I can't imagine that they've left.'' McHenry looked around their little camp. Totten had crept from behind his rock and was sitting on his heels looking over at Peggy and Winslow. ''Ever see anybody so useless?'' he asked Falwell.

''He's the one who belongs in Chicago, not you.''

McHenry looked over at Jeremy, who was sitting cross-legged next to the cliff face. His body was slumped, but his eyes darted back and forth, peering from beneath the hat brim. McHenry could imagine what was going through the frightened boy's mind.

McHenry saw that Austin had recovered his rifle and was sitting next to a rock, leaning against it. He was staring at the body of the bandit, which wasn't a good sign. After looking around at the weapons scattered on the ground, McHenry told the boy, ''It's time you got yourself a grown-up's weapon. Grab Winslow's carbine there and hand your rifle to Jeremy.''

''Okay,'' Austin said eagerly. He got to his feet, bent down, and hustled over to the carbine on the ground. He picked that up and then scampered over to Jeremy.

Jeremy sat up and reached eagerly for Austin's rifle.

''Thanks,'' he said. ''I'm gonna shoot as good as you do. You'll see.''

''You'll never hit anything, but they won't know that. Just make lots of noise. That'll scare 'em. Here, take my bullets.''

McHenry looked at Falwell. ''And how are you fixed for ammunition?''

''Well, I'd feel better with a lot more. That was quite a pack of Apaches we ran into.''

McHenry took off one of the bandoliers he was wearing and started transferring cartridges to the other one. ''I used up a bunch attacking those bandits in camp, and I didn't find that many more in their camp.'' He jerked a thumb at the dead outlaw. ''We can get some from the hombre lying over there.'' He pointed a finger toward the open desert. ''But we'd better try to scavenge what we can from the two bandits out there.''

''Good idea.''

McHenry wiped a hand over his face. ''It's hot,'' he said. There was no shade anymore. The sun had risen high enough to burn down directly on every spot where the little party was huddled. "And it's going to get hotter. We'll have to conserve the water."

"I think we should move to some other spot." Falwell mopped his brow.

"And how are we going to move with Winslow wounded like that?"

Falwell slid closer and whispered, "This is not a good place to fight off Apaches."

"These rocks make as good a cover as we'll find." As Falwell pointed skyward, McHenry studied the tops of the cliffs. "There's no overhang," he said, recognizing the danger too. "Apaches can be like mountain goats. You're thinking they may get above us."

"Exactly." Falwell turned and looked up the cliff face too. "Even if they can't lean over far enough to get a good shot at us, they could still just roll down rocks on us."

"Well, maybe we'll be lucky and there won't be any rocks up on top," McHenry said. "But where else could we go?"

"There were some spots farther back the way we came. They had sufficient overhang so that we wouldn't have to worry about the Apaches getting above us."

"Okay, you make sense," McHenry said. "But first we have to get the guns and ammunition from those two dead bandits out there."

"You go for one and I for the other."

"How about if I go after them one at a time and you cover me?"

"I was as fast as you coming out of that canyon."

McHenry smiled weakly. "We both had real good reason not to be last in line. But I think you're a better shot than I am, and I'm going to be busy with the guns and ammunition. You watch the cliffs and the sagebrush." Then he looked over at Austin and Jeremy. "Okay, boys, here's your chance to do a man's job."

The boys got to their feet and, bending over, hurried to McHenry. "What do you want us to do?"

He pointed out to the desert. "I'm going out there to get the weapons of those two outlaws we killed, and I want you to cover me with your guns. Get over behind those two rocks."

The boys hurried to their positions.

McHenry looked once more at the desert and the cliffs. Then he jumped to his feet and ran straight out. Without a glance back, he ran until he was able to leap to a sliding stop next to the body of the dead bandit. He turned himself around, brought his Winchester to bear on the cliffs, and waited for a response from the Apaches. The rocks on top were beginning to shimmer in the heat waves rising from them. But no man was visible.

The bandit wore a bandolier of ammunition. Also, he had a pistol stuck in his belt and was lying on top of a carbine. McHenry rolled him over first to get at the carbine and the pistol. Then he struggled to pull the bandolier over the bandit's head. As an afterthought, he also picked up the man's wide-brimmed sombrero.

Next he scanned the cliffs and the desert around him again. Still no movement. He looked at those who were covering him. Falwell nodded. McHenry jumped to his feet and dashed for the cliff.

At any second he expected a slug to stop him or to kick up sand in front of him. But there was nothing. He reached the rocks, jumped over the fallen bandit leader, and crashed to an awkward stop on the ground.

Totten cringed away from him.

McHenry rolled over and sat up. He tossed the pistol to Totten, who caught it clumsily. "Use it," McHenry ordered. "It might save your life soon. And the lives of all the rest of us."

Totten nodded and held the gun with both hands. He walked on his knees to the nearest rock and peered over it.

McHenry didn't think the pistol was going to do the man any good. There was just something missing in Totten.

McHenry got to his feet and scurried over to Falwell. He dumped the carbine and bandolier at his feet. "That will help," he said as he started over to Peggy.

She was cradling her father's head in her lap. He was resting quietly. Her back was arched in a curve to provide his face some shade. The white flesh of her neck was exposed to the fierce sun.

"Here," McHenry said, and he plunked the sombrero on her head. It was much too large for her, so he tipped it back and let it rest there loosely.

She turned to look at him, puzzled.

He smiled. "You'll be red as a hot branding iron if you don't have shade."

She nodded. "Thank you," she whispered.

The hat came down to her eyebrows and covered her ears, and she looked comical to McHenry. If there had not been so much pain visible in her face, he would have laughed.

"You're welcome," he replied.

"Do you think the Apaches are gone?"

McHenry hesitated, then shook his head slowly. "No, not yet. But there's no telling when they'll decide to leave. If they get spooked, they could vanish instantly, whether we're here or not."

"But they're still out there now?"

"I think so."

"When will this all stop?"

"You mean the Apaches?"

"No. Look at Austin over there."

Austin was crouched behind a large rock. He held a Winchester carbine and looked ready to use it.

"He's a boy," Peggy said. "And he shot a man."

"He shot a bandit who would have gotten us all killed. I'm mighty grateful to him. I would have expected a man to do the same."

"But he's not a man. He's still just a boy."

"Boys have to grow up fast out here."

"That's too fast," Peggy said. "He still needs time to be a boy. He and Jeremy both."

"Well. . . ."

"I know. It's a hard country. That's what you were going to say, wasn't it?"

"It is hard. I don't like it that way, ma'am, but that's the way it is."

"That has to change."

"Yes, but how?" McHenry asked. "I haven't noticed any change as long as I can remember."

"Hey, McHenry!" Falwell called. "I'd feel better if you went and got the ammunition from that other bandit. The Apaches won't wait forever."

"Right." McHenry turned to Peggy. "I'm sorry for the way things are, but there's nothing that I can do about it. Except move to Chicago, I guess."

"I'm not blaming you," Peggy murmured. "I didn't mean it that way."

"I know. I don't know who is to blame. It's just the way things are."

He turned and got down behind the rock. Then he ran along the cliff face toward where the second bandit had fallen. He scampered from rock to rock or merely hugged the sheer cliff. He could feel the warmth of the rocks against his back. Soon they would be too hot to touch.

He kept going. He hadn't realized just how far it was to the fallen outlaw. He even began to think the bandit wasn't there anymore. Had the man been alive and gotten up and walked away? But that didn't seem likely. Had the Apaches run off with the body? That seemed equally unlikely. The Apaches had no reason to carry off a dead body.

Finally he reached the bandit at the base of the cliff. A carbine lay nearby. And the bandit had actually worn a holster for his pistol.

McHenry unbuckled the holster and slid it out from underneath the body. He buckled it again to make it easier to carry. He searched the man's pockets for cartridges, found about a dozen, and stuffed them into his pocket. He picked up the carbine and gun belt and turned to go.

Not until he looked up did he realize that there had been a dip in the trail to this spot, and now he couldn't see the camp or Falwell and his Winchester.

So Falwell couldn't see him.

And neither of them saw the two Apaches coming up behind McHenry.

Chapter Seven

O NE of the Apaches barked at McHenry, and he froze in ·terror. When no bullets hit him, he slowly craned his head around. The two Apaches stood ten feet behind him with their carbines pointed at him. They could have shot him easily. McHenry realized that they meant to take him alive, the worst of all possible fates.

And he was in a helpless predicament through his own carelessness. His right hand was carrying the bandit's pistol and its holster, and the other hand held two carbines by their barrels. There was no way he could get a finger on a trigger quickly. Both Apaches could instantly put a bullet into him if he tried to use a weapon.

The Apaches started walking forward slowly. One of them pointed to what McHenry was carrying and motioned him to drop them.

McHenry knew instinctively not to go meekly with the two Indians; death was preferable. However, their desire to take him alive might still give him a fighting chance at survival.

"Falwell!" McHenry yelled, and he swung the carbines up by the barrels and hurled them toward one Apache and the holster toward the other. Then he went for his pistol.

The Apaches easily batted away the objects thrown at them, and they leaped for McHenry. They collided with him just as he had his pistol out of his holster. He dropped the weapon and all three went down in a pile. The Apaches dropped their carbines and tried to pin his arms and encircle his neck.

"Falwell!" McHenry screamed again. He wrestled with the men, but this was not like his earlier encounter the night before. There had been only one man then, and two Apaches were one Apache too many.

They jerked him to his feet. One Apache had a handful of McHenry's hair, and McHenry could feel hairs being pulled out by the roots. Each Indian had a strong grip on his arms, pinning them back. One man clamped a hand over his mouth. McHenry lashed out with his legs, but they kicked him hard and forced his arms so far back that he feared they would pop from their sockets.

As one Apache let go of McHenry, the other grabbed both of his arms. McHenry tried to buck the man off, then twirled around to shake him loose. But the other Apache had let go in order to grab a Winchester. McHenry's world spun when the Apache smashed his head with it.

McHenry didn't lose consciousness, but he was

dizzy and felt helpless. While one Apache held him tight, the other scooped up the weapons quickly. With one hand cradling all the weapons, including four Winchesters now, the second Apache helped shove McHenry farther down the trail.

McHenry made a panic lurch to the side and drove the Apache holding his arms against the cliff. The man's head bounced off the rock, and as his grip faltered, McHenry shook him loose. The Apache staggered a step and crumpled to the ground.

McHenry drove a fist into the face of the other Apache, and that man released his one-hand grip on him. All the weapons clattered to the ground. McHenry now drove a boot into the man's chest, sending him sprawling.

McHenry fell down too. He was still dizzy from the blow on the head. But he got to his knees, grabbed a Winchester, cocked the hammer and brought up the barrel. Too late.

The carbine fired, but the Indian leaped right past the gun and knocked him over on his back. McHenry felt as if his legs were going to break backward.

The Apache rolled on the ground and jumped to his feet with a knife in his hand. He screamed and leaped for McHenry. McHenry parried the knife thrust with the carbine, knocking the man's knife hand over his head. But McHenry had to let go of the carbine to grab the knife hand.

They rolled and rolled. They rolled into the cliff and

then rolled away in the other directions. Both men had both hands on the knife or the Apache's knife hand, jerking one way or the other to loosen the grip of the other man.

They bounced up against a rock. Still clutching desperately to the knife, the men rose to their feet. They shoved about, each trying to throw the other off balance, first one way and then the other, each knowing that the first man to let go of the knife would be dead.

A shot rang out. The Apache's head snapped back and his mouth flew open. McHenry froze, and he felt the Apache's hands go limp. Then the man's entire body collapsed. The knife fell on the ground.

McHenry looked up to see Falwell levering another cartridge into his Winchester.

"I started after you when you disappeared from sight," Falwell explained. "Then, when I heard the carbine go off, I started running."

McHenry nodded, out of breath, shaking from fright. "Not a second too soon. That guy was strong. Thanks." While he took a couple of deep breaths, Falwell came forward and started picking up weapons. McHenry joined him. "You didn't hear me call for you?"

"Nope."

"These canyons sure do funny things to sounds. I was yelling as loud as I could." He had his arms full of weapons, but this time he kept a tight grip on his own Winchester with the finger on the trigger. "Let's go."

They headed up the path back toward their camp.

"Wait a second," McHenry said, and he raised his Winchester with one hand and took careful aim at the unconscious Apache lying near the cliff face. But the carbine hung there in the air.

"You going to shoot him?" Falwell asked casually.

"That'll be one less coming after us later."

"Makes sense."

McHenry sighted down the barrel. Seconds passed.

"What are you waiting for?" Falwell asked.

"I don't know. I guess I'm bothered by what Peggy Winslow would think of this."

Falwell looked at the unconscious Apache lying in the dirt. "How are you going to feel if he kills her an hour from now?"

"I know." The Winchester continued to waver. "This just seems—" A couple of more seconds. Then one shot and the Apache's head jerked.

"Okay," Falwell said. "Let's get back."

Falwell headed up the trail. McHenry stared for a few moments at the Apache he had just shot. Then he clenched his teeth, sighed, and strode after Falwell.

"That woman's getting to you, isn't she?" Falwell said over his shoulder.

"Yeah, I guess so."

"She's beautiful and has strong principles. She'd get to any man."

"You?" McHenry asked.

He couldn't see Falwell's smile, but he caught the tone of his voice when Falwell said, "I can picture her on my arm at a ball in Washington. She'd turn heads all right. Probably lecture some generals too."

McHenry chuckled. Yes, he, too, could picture that.

Falwell stopped and gasped, "The camp! There's—"

McHenry and Falwell both dropped what they were carrying except for their own carbines. About eight Apaches were descending on their little camp. Several were already in the camp, and the rest would reach it in seconds.

McHenry and Falwell started firing. They couldn't shoot into the camp itself for fear of hitting their own people, but they each fired a couple of shots at the Apaches who hadn't reached the camp yet. All of their hurried shots missed their targets.

The Apaches who hadn't reached the camp yet slid to a stop. They fired back, and their aim was as poor as McHenry's and Falwell's.

"Keep shooting, Falwell!" McHenry said. "Chase off the ones in the rear. I'm heading for the camp."

Falwell stepped to the side to rest his carbine on a rock for a better aim. He started firing again.

McHenry broke into an all-out run. It was hard running on the desert soil, but every second would count. He watched the attack on the camp helplessly.

Winslow was actually on his feet and wrestling with one Indian, but about all he could do in his badly wounded state was to hang on and keep the Apache from using his carbine.

Totten fired his pistol once at the nearest Apache, but he missed. The Apache ran right into him and knocked him flat. Totten scrambled to his knees. He dropped his pistol and put up his hands in surrender. Then he folded them and began begging for mercy. The Apache was going to shoot him but hesitated, as if confused by Totten's action. Then the Apache drew his knife and made one slash with a wide thrust of his arm. He didn't even watch as a horrified Totten clutched at his throat and slowly pitched face forward to the ground.

Austin got off several shots, and Jeremy one. Both of them missed the attackers. The Apache with the knife lunged at Austin, but the boy dropped the carbine and scampered to the side. The Apache sheathed his knife, kept the carbine in one hand, and grabbed Peggy around the waist with the other hand and started hauling her out of the camp.

She screamed, and Winslow yelled, but he couldn't break free from the Apache he was struggling with. Austin and Jeremy leaped on the Apache holding Peggy. Austin threw his arms tightly around the Apache's neck and Jeremy tackled him around the legs. Peggy beat at the man with her fists. The Apache was thrown off balance, and all four people crashed down. The Apache lost his carbine.

Winslow was thrown to the ground by the Apache

he was wrestling with. The Indian fired his carbine and fired a slug into Winslow's side. Winslow jerked and lay still. The Apache went after the group fighting on the ground. Peggy screamed again.

Winslow stirred. He rolled on his side and picked up Totten's pistol. He cocked the pistol, pointed it at the Apache still standing, and fired.

The Apache jerked upright and dropped his Winchester. He staggered forward and fell against a rock. He tried to get up. Winslow fired another shot into him, and the Indian rolled to the ground. Winslow tried to aim the pistol at the Apache holding his daughter, but Austin and Jeremy were in the way. He collapsed in pain. Unable to keep the pistol up, he took a couple of deep breaths, rolled over on his stomach, and started crawling toward Peggy and the others, the pistol still in his hand.

The other Apache kicked Jeremy off. Then he fumbled for his sheath knife and slashed at Austin, catching him in the arm. Austin screamed and let go.

The Apache got to his knees. Peggy was thrashing in his grip as he tried to get to his feet. Jeremy ran into him again, knocking him and Peggy back to the ground. The Apache kicked at him.

Austin found his Winchester again. The Apache saw it, let go of Peggy and his knife at the same time, and reached for his own carbine.

Winslow fired at him. In his pain and with an unsteady hand, he missed, but the Apache jumped back.

He fired one quick shot at Austin but missed too. He would have fired at Winslow also, but he heard McHenry's running feet.

The Apache turned. McHenry fired on the run, shooting from the hip with his carbine. The bullet grazed the Apache and spoiled his aim. His bullet whizzed past McHenry.

McHenry levered in another cartridge as he stopped. He was a little quicker than the Apache, and his next bullet was on its way before the Apache finished working the lever of his carbine. This bullet hit the man in the side and turned him halfway round.

As the Apache tried to get around the rock, Austin fired at him again, from only ten feet away. The bullet lodged in the Apache's right arm, and he grunted and dropped the carbine. McHenry fired once more, and the Indian went down.

McHenry ran forward. A glance told him that the other Apache lying there was dead. He raised his carbine to help Falwell chase off the other Apaches retreating along the cliff face among the rocks. Finally he stopped shooting. Falwell arrived shortly thereafter.

McHenry rushed to Peggy's side. She was lying on the ground with her hands shielding her face. "They're gone," he said.

She parted her hands and looked up at him. "My father?" she asked.

McHenry looked over at Winslow, who lay facedown in the dirt. "Come on," he said. He helped

Peggy to her feet and they joined Falwell. Falwell rolled over the limp figure.

"Father?" she said.

Winslow opened his eyes and shook his head. "I think this is the end."

"No, no!" she cried.

McHenry checked the new wound. Peggy was already tearing a strip of cloth from her petticoat.

"This is a flesh wound," McHenry said. "Lots of blood, but no vital organs were hit."

Winslow groaned. "I can't lose blood forever."

Peggy pressed the cloth to the new wound. "You just lie still, Father. The more you move around, the more blood you'll lose."

Austin tapped McHenry on the shoulder. The boy had a hand clamped over his forearm and his brow was furrowed. Some blood dripped off his fingers. Jeremy was standing next to him. He looked worried too. "Austin's hurt, Mr. McHenry," Jeremy said.

McHenry reached for the wound. "Bullet?" he asked.

Austin shook his head. "That Apache cut me with his knife."

McHenry turned toward Peggy. "Could you come up with another bandage for a brave young man?"

Peggy complied quickly. McHenry rolled up the boy's sleeve and wrapped the cloth tightly around the wound. "You'll have a scar there for the rest of your

life, Austin,'' he said. ''You'll love telling your grand-
children about how you got that wound.''

Austin snorted. ''Mr. McHenry, I don't think I'm
gonna live long enough to have any children. There's
still a lot of Apaches out there.''

McHenry patted him on the back. ''We'll get out of
here, all right. Don't forget about Mitch and that Army
patrol.''

''Mr. McHenry?'' Jeremy asked. ''Was I brave
too?''

McHenry nodded. ''I saw you jump on that Apache.
I'd say you both did a man's job today.''

Jeremy smiled. Austin held on to his wound and
stood a little straighter.

McHenry stepped over to Totten. Gently he raised
the man by one shoulder. Totten was already dead. He
let the body back down.

Crouching behind a rock, McHenry scanned the desert in front of them. He took off his hat and wiped the
sweat from his brow. He put his hat back on and scrutinized the cliff tops. They would be sitting ducks for
anybody up there.

Falwell joined McHenry behind the rock and said,
''We're in a bad fix here.''

McHenry nodded. ''I don't think we scared them
off. There's still probably close to twenty of them.''

''I winged two of them as they were running away,
but not bad enough to put them out of action.''

"Winslow can't be moved. He'll just bleed to death on the way. He has to lie still."

Falwell stared up at the cliff top. "Maybe they won't go up there. They haven't yet." He looked out at the desert. "There's enough of them that they just might decide to sit out there, keep us pinned down, and then rush us again. They know what to expect now."

A bullet ricocheted off the rock and dug itself into the ground right next to McHenry's knee. Both stared wide-eyed at the bullet crater in the dirt.

"That came straight down," McHenry said.

They looked up at the cliff top above. An Apache stuck his head over and pointed a carbine. Another shot was fired. This one splattered itself flat next to Falwell's head.

Both men fired their Winchesters at him, but the Apache had ducked back out of sight. Then they jumped up and hurried to the cliff face.

"Austin, Jeremy!" McHenry called. "Over against the wall!"

The two men and both boys pressed themselves against the cliff.

Peggy motioned to them. "Quick, move my father out of the way against the cliff."

Without hesitation, McHenry and Falwell dropped their Winchesters and lunged forward. They grabbed Winslow by the arms and legs and hauled him over to the rock. Winslow groaned and grimaced. When they had settled him against the rock, Peggy took her place beside him. She squinted at the sun as she searched the cliff tops. She had lost the sombrero.

Another Indian stuck his head over the edge and fired down at them. The shot was hurried, and the bullet plunked into the sand six feet from anybody.

Winslow said without opening his eyes, "You must all leave here."

"I don't think you can be moved," McHenry told him.

"I'm dying anyway. Leave me here. It won't be long."

"Father!" Peggy snapped. "Don't you talk like that!"

"McHenry, you know it's true," Winslow urged.

"We won't leave you, Mr. Winslow," McHenry said.

"We could try to carry you," Falwell suggested. "We don't have a stretcher or any way of making one, but McHenry and I could support you between us."

"That'll be too slow," Winslow said. "You'll be able to move faster without me along."

"Father, stop talking like that." Peggy was almost screaming.

"I love you with all my life," Winslow said. "You are more precious to me than life itself. Leave me here. Go. Save yourself. For *my* sake. I won't be the cause of your death. I should never have brought you out here in the first place."

Peggy put her hand over his mouth. "I won't listen to that anymore. I won't leave you."

Another bullet chunked into the ground near Jeremy. He pulled his legs in tighter against the wall.

"Well," McHenry said, "let's give it a try. We can't stay here."

He and Falwell got to their feet, and they each put a hand under one of Winslow's armpits. Peggy helped, and they got Winslow to his feet, but he couldn't stand by himself.

"Miss Winslow," McHenry said, "put your father's arms over our shoulders. And stick his pistol in my belt. We may need it."

Peggy nodded. She helped get Winslow's arms over the shoulders of the two men, then picked up Winslow's pistol and thrust it into McHenry's belt.

McHenry told Austin and Jeremy, "Boys, you grab all the canteens and the saddlebag with the food. Keep a sharp eye for any Apache sticking his head over the top. Shoot at anything you see moving up there."

"Okay," Austin said. Both boys jumped to their feet. They gathered up the canteens and slung them over their shoulders. Austin grabbed the saddlebag. They huddled close to the men and held their guns pointing upward.

McHenry and Falwell led off to the left. As they hesitated at the line of rocks they had hidden behind, Falwell suggested, "Let's make it to those rocks right over there."

"Good," McHenry agreed. "Let's go."

They stepped out into the open. Winslow was dead-weight between them. He couldn't walk, and each man felt his fingers digging into them from the pain.

"Behind us!" Austin shouted.

McHenry looked back quickly. Several Apaches had appeared in the rocks some distance away on the other side of the camp. Shots started coming their way, plinking off the rocks around them or chunking into the dirt.

"Hurry!" McHenry shouted. "Into those rocks ahead, boys!" He and Falwell began to almost run, dragging Winslow's feet behind them.

Austin and Jeremy dashed ahead, canteens clunking and banging against their bodies, and with the saddlebag flopping wildly. They ducked behind some rocks and then poked their weapons over the top. Each fired a shot.

McHenry motioned his head toward Peggy. "You too," he said. "Run on ahead. We'll catch up."

"I'm staying with my father," she insisted.

Falwell cried, "You aren't doing him any good here!"

"I won't leave!"

McHenry muttered and glared at her. A bullet whizzed past his ears close enough for him to hear it. With the butt of his carbine he thumped Peggy in the middle of her back. She flinched and gasped.

"Don't be so stubborn!" he shouted. "You're making things worse. Run!"

Peggy looked at him in fright and humiliation. But she turned and scampered ahead and took cover behind some rocks beyond Austin and Jeremy.

McHenry and Falwell reached the first rocks and let Winslow down hurriedly. Peggy started to get up to run back to where they were. "Stay there!" McHenry shouted angrily. He and Falwell took cover themselves and started returning fire.

"McHenry," Winslow said, "give me my gun."

McHenry looked at him doubtfully. "Can you shoot?"

"Yes, yes, please!"

"Okay. Every gun will help. Here, slide up over this way."

He helped Winslow up to the rock and over to its edge. He took the pistol from his belt and handed it to Winslow. "Good luck."

"Thanks. Do you really think you can get my daughter out of here alive?"

"I'm not sure any of us are going to get out alive, but if *I* do, *she* will too. I can promise you that."

Winslow nodded slightly. "That's good enough, McHenry."

McHenry looked back at the attacking Apaches. They were sneaking closer but weren't making a charge. He fired another shot and again levered the carbine, which had a single cartridge left. He started taking others from the bandolier and stuffing them into the gate on the cheek of the carbine. There were many empty loops in the bandolier now.

''She's a fine young woman,'' Winslow told McHenry.

McHenry paused in his firing and looked down at Winslow. ''That she is, sir. You can be very proud of her.''

''I am, and I love her with all my heart.''

''We'll get her out of here, or I'll die trying.''

The Apaches had settled in behind rocks, and there was seldom a good target. McHenry fired at a leg he could see. The leg was jerked back out of sight. He heard Winslow cock the pistol and fire a shot. And then Peggy screamed and ran toward him. She was sobbing uncontrollably. Winslow had shot himself in the head.

Chapter Eight

Mc HENRY looked at Winslow and then at Peggy in shock. But before he could do anything, another bullet smashed into the rock he was crouching behind. He ducked and then brought up the Winchester and fired. Angry, he fired again and again.

"Take it easy!" Falwell shouted at him. "You're not shooting at anything. Save the ammunition."

McHenry lowered the Winchester and took a couple of deep breaths. Then, as he looked down at Winslow, his anger diminished and was replaced by sadness and resignation.

Peggy was still sobbing on top of her father. McHenry rested the Winchester against the rock and crawled toward her amid the crunch of the empty shell casings on the ground. His bandolier was almost empty, and his gun belt didn't have a full supply of cartridges.

"Miss Winslow," he whispered, gently touching her arm.

She slowly turned, fighting back the sobs. Tears

119

washed down her cheeks. "Why?" she asked. "Why did he do it?"

"Because he loved you."

"What?" she sobbed. "That's—that's crazy."

McHenry shook his head slowly. "He knew he was dying, but he also knew it might take a day or two and we couldn't sit here for that long. He realized he was slowing us down, and he didn't want you to stay here and wait."

"We could have taken him with us," Peggy insisted. The tears continued to flow.

"Look at his shirt, Miss Winslow. Look how much blood he's lost. And he was also bleeding inside. Every movement, every step we took pumped more blood."

Peggy sat up and plopped against the rock. Her head sagged and she rocked back and forth. She kept sobbing.

McHenry felt completely helpless. Having decided that there was nothing more he could do at the moment, he got back to his firing position.

"A brave man, that Eli Winslow," Falwell observed.

"Yeah," McHenry said forlornly, and he turned his attention back to the Apaches.

McHenry and Falwell fired less frequently now, finding the elusive Apaches hard to spot, much less hit. The Apaches were not coming closer, but simply standing off and exchanging gunfire. They never fired from the same place twice, whereas McHenry and Falwell had no place else to go. And Austin and Jeremy fired only occasionally. They were never fast enough to get a bead on an Apache before he had ducked out of sight again.

Falwell stopped shooting, brought the Winchester back, huddled lower behind the rock, and said, ''I think they've gone.''

McHenry's eyes scanned all the rocks. Not a sign of them. No shooting. ''Well, maybe for now.'' He sat down on the ground and studied their surroundings. There were fewer and smaller rocks here than back where they had been. And here the canyon wall had not only receded but it also sloped gradually up to the top in what was almost a gully.

He looked at Falwell and nodded to the hill. Falwell nodded back and said, ''They could sit up there and pick us off at leisure, once they get over here from the other cliff.''

''We have to go on immediately,'' McHenry said. ''We can't stay here.''

Peggy was leaning back against the rock. The blinding sun was full in her face, but she didn't care. Her body was limp.

''We have to move on,'' McHenry told her.

''No! I'll not leave my father.''

He wished he could find the right words, not words that would sting and hurt. ''Miss Winslow, your father is dead.''

''No, he can't be.'' She started sobbing again.

"He is. He wanted it that way. He knew what he was doing. He didn't want to burden you."

Jeremy crept close to her. He tugged at her dress sleeve and said, "I know how you feel, ma'am. I saw my pa killed yesterday. By the Apaches."

Peggy fought back her sobs. She brought her head erect and gazed at Jeremy. She lifted a hand and put it on his shoulder. She wanted to speak, but she couldn't. She just nodded.

Jeremy went on, "I know my pa's dead, and you have to know your pa's dead too. I don't like my pa dead." He stifled a sob and wiped away a single tear. "But that's the way it is. And my pa would want me to go on. I know he would. And your pa wants *you* to go on. I know that."

Peggy looked at the boy, tears in her eyes, her brow furrowed, her mouth turned down. "You seem so grown-up already," she said softly.

Jeremy snuggled in closer to her. "I don't feel so grown-up." He looked at McHenry and smiled a little. "Even if I'm doin' a man's job today."

McHenry smiled as he patted the boy on the shoulder.

Peggy wrapped an arm around Jeremy. "Mr. McHenry," she said, "I want to give my father a decent Christian burial before we leave."

He sighed. "We don't have time. We don't even have the tools."

Peggy stared at him. "Do you expect me to just

leave his body lying here in the sun, free for the Apaches and scavengers to molest?''

''Think about what your father would have wanted. He would want you to leave immediately. I promise you we'll come back when it's safe and give him a decent burial. I promise.''

''Me too,'' Falwell said. ''We can't remain here. Look around you. We could stay crouched behind these rocks for now, but soon the Apaches will find that opening in the canyon wall behind us, and then we'll have no place to hide. No place whatsoever. We must leave now.''

Peggy looked from one man to the other. ''You'll bring me with you when you come back?''

''Of course,'' they said together.

She wiped the tears from her eyes. ''All right.'' She smiled down at Jeremy. ''Thank you, my young friend.''

Jeremy squeezed her hand. ''I like you, Miss Winslow.''

''I like you too. So let's get out of this canyon and back to town so we can enjoy each other's company better.''

''Yeah,'' Jeremy said with a big smile.

She looked at Austin and said, ''You too.''

Austin smiled shyly. ''Aw,'' he mumbled.

McHenry stuffed cartridges into the gate of his carbine until the magazine was full. ''There's no telling what the Apaches are up to,'' he told Falwell. ''But they seem to have withdrawn for now. They probably have at least one scout watching us, but that doesn't mean they'll attack if we start to move. They have their own timetable.''

Falwell scanned the rocks but saw no sign of Apaches. ''It's hot, but the place I have in mind may have some shade, and it's not too far back down the canyon.''

McHenry stood up. ''Let's go. Boys, got the canteens and the food?''

''Yep,'' they said eagerly.

''Falwell, you lead since you know the spot you're heading for.''

''Fine with me. And you bring up the rear.'' Falwell started forward. ''Come on, boys. Let's find some shade.''

McHenry helped Peggy to her feet, saying, ''I want you to know how much I admire your father. I envy his courage and his devotion.''

She touched his arm. ''Thank you. He liked you too.'' She started after Falwell and the boys.

McHenry bent down, picked up Winslow's hat, and called out, ''You lost your sombrero.'' He walked up to her and offered her Winslow's hat. ''I think your father would be pleased if you wore his hat. He'd want to protect you from the sun as well as from Apaches.''

She smiled at him as she accepted the hat and held it to her bosom. ''Thank you.'' When she put it on her head, it, too, slipped down to her ears. She tipped it back so that she could see. She smiled again. "Reminds me of when I was a little girl."

McHenry smiled too, but he didn't say anything. Peggy turned and started walking. He followed, constantly stopping to look back and scan the rocks and the desert. No Apache appeared.

They walked for about two hours until they found the spot that Falwell had in mind. The canyon wall here had a distinct bulge to it, and no one atop the cliff would be able to see the foot of it. And the cliff had been shattered so often that its base was cluttered with huge slabs and rocks. There was plenty of cover.

The small party dropped into the camp with relief. Falwell had been right. The rocks and the slabs were high enough, and with the sun now descending in the sky, everyone could sit in the shade. It was a welcome respite from the direct sunlight.

McHenry passed around the beef jerky, and each person had one piece. They each worked hard to chew up a handful of uncooked beans. A long drink from a canteen washed it all down. Then they settled in to wait.

Ultimately, the sun dropped behind the far canyon wall and plunged the entire canyon into shadow. Night seemed to descend rapidly after that. Falwell and McHenry both kept guard. The boys lay down near the cliff face and used their hats as pillows. They lay there with their eyes open, though. Sleep didn't come easily under the circumstances.

Peggy came up and sat down beside McHenry. She looked out into the darkness. "Mr. McHenry, what are you planning to do? When will the Apaches attack again?"

He shrugged. "The Apaches will attack when they feel like it. Probably not at night, but you can't be sure. And we can't be sure that they haven't already left because they're usually raiders. They hit the stage station but haven't run yet. They must be getting awful itchy to ride off."

"Do we wait here?"

"That's my idea for now. This spot will be as easy to defend as any I can think of in the canyon. And if we wait out the Apaches, they'll simply quit and leave. There will always be more prey for them."

"What about Mitch? Do you think he found that Army patrol?"

McHenry nodded toward the desert. "If he did and he comes down this canyon looking for us, we should be able to spot him from here. We can see all the way across the canyon."

"You like Mitch, don't you?"

"Yeah, I like him a lot. He's been a good friend." He looked at her. "I know what you're thinking. Well, I know he made it."

She just nodded, but he knew she shared his doubts.

Peggy looked at the two boys lying nearby. "What will happen to them when we get back?"

He thought about that for a moment, and then he said to Austin, "You got any kin nearby?"

"We don't have any kin anywhere."

McHenry frowned. "What, no uncles and aunts anywhere?"

"Nope."

"Grandparents, cousins, anybody?"

"Nope. Where will Jeremy and me go?"

"Maybe the stage company will know what to do."

"Will they send us to an orphanage?"

The thought made McHenry shudder inside. "I'll make sure there's something better for you."

Jeremy looked up now. "Could we just stay with you, Mr. McHenry?"

"In Chicago?"

"I don't want to go to Chicago." Austin shook his head. "I want to stay here."

"Yeah, me too," Jeremy said. "Well, never mind, Mr. McHenry."

McHenry looked chagrined. Peggy smiled and laughed silently. Then she went over and sat down near the boys. "I think we should all try to get some sleep." she said.

"Can we come closer to you?" Jeremy asked.

"Sure."

The boys scooted over next to Peggy, one on each side, and they all lay down.

Falwell stirred and came over to McHenry. "I heard something moving out there," he said.

McHenry gritted his teeth. ''I was really hoping that they'd given up on us.''

Falwell poked a finger toward the desert. ''Straight out. Sounds like a couple of them walking directly toward us. Listen.''

McHenry strained to pick up sounds in the desert, and soon he heard footsteps crunching on the dirt, and then a stone clinking. He pulled back the hammer of the Winchester as he glanced back at the three people curled up near the cliff face. He decided he'd let the first shot alert them because all they could do in the meantime was worry.

Falwell moved off to the left to another rock slab. They sighted down the barrels of the carbines. There was little besides darkness and shadows to aim at. But the sounds were getting louder.

''Must be a bunch of them,'' Falwell whispered. ''Almost like they're going to charge en masse.''

McHenry could now make out shapes in the darkness. The figures stopped, then started forward again. He drew a bead on the one in front.

It was a shadowy figure, and very tall. He waited, trying to get a better idea of whom he was going to shoot at.

Falwell lowered his carbine suddenly, and he cried under his breath, ''Those aren't Apaches!''

Then McHenry recognized them too. "Well, I'll be," he said.

In front of them the first horse pricked up its ears and snuffled once.

"It's those runaway Mexican horses."

Chapter Nine

FALWELL scampered over to McHenry, whose eyes were riveted on the three horses standing in front of them. The foremost horse had pricked up its ears again, and its muzzle was testing the wind.

"These three must have gotten lonesome," McHenry said.

Falwell chuckled. "Maybe that one in front wants his daily sugar ration or something. We got some horses back at the fort that act like puppies."

"And the others tagged along just because horses like to be together." McHenry peered into the darkness past the horses. "Still," he said slowly, "why didn't the Apaches grab these mounts? They like horses even better than they like killing white people."

"Maybe they just didn't see these."

"How could they miss them? They must be watching us. Unless—" McHenry clapped a hand over his own mouth; he didn't want to get his hopes up.

"Unless what?"

"Unless the Apaches are gone."

"It makes sense," Falwell agreed. "That's why they

didn't attack us while we were moving to this spot. That last attack was their last effort. Tried their best and then vamoosed.''

"If we grab these horses, we could all mount and get out of here too. We'd have to double up, but that won't be much of a burden to the critters. We still got some water and a little bit of food, and we could ride all the way back to the last town.'' McHenry was excited by the prospect.

Falwell didn't hesitate. "I'm with you," he said.

They stepped away from their hiding places and started slowly forward. The horse in front lowered its head, snuffled, and took a step toward them. It was an easy task for McHenry to grasp its reins. He patted the horse on the neck. "Nice fellow. Come on, boy. Let's grab your friends.''

The other horses were less friendly, but they offered no resistance to the grabbing of their reins.

While Falwell held all the reins, McHenry hurried back to Peggy and the boys and woke them up.

Peggy sat upright, startled. "What's wrong? Are the Apaches coming again?''

"We caught some horses, and we're going to ride out of here before the Apaches know we're gone. In fact, they may not even be here anymore.''

Peggy leaped to her feet and picked up her father's hat and put it on.

McHenry said to the boys, "You grab the canteens

and your guns." He pulled over the saddlebag with the food. "I'll take this. Come on, let's go."

The four of them gathered their things and hurried to where Falwell was holding the horses. McHenry asked, "Have you heard anything?"

"Just the breeze."

"Good." He turned to Peggy. "Can you ride a horse?"

"Hardly at all. But you just watch me learn real quick."

McHenry smiled. "You'll be okay." He grabbed a set of reins. "Here, you ride this one."

Peggy tried awkwardly to mount the horse. The step to the stirrup was high for her. After a few attempts, McHenry finally put a hand under her seat and boosted her up. Startled at the familiarity, she looked back at him disapprovingly. "Sorry," he said, "but this is no time to worry about manners." He handed her the reins. "Keep a good grip on them, don't leave any slack, and keep your knees pressed tightly to his sides."

Peggy nodded. "I've got it." As she pulled the reins taut, the horse shook its head up and down. "Whoa, boy, whoa."

Falwell had already mounted a horse, and he held out a set of reins to McHenry, saying, "You take Austin and I'll take Jeremy."

"I don't need any help," Jeremy said, handing the

canteens to McHenry. Then he advanced to Falwell's horse and reached for the stirrup.

Austin scoffed. "Jeremy, shut up," he said. "Let Mr. McHenry help you up there."

McHenry didn't wait. He dropped the canteens and lifted the boy up behind Falwell. Then he handed the boy his rifle and said, "Hang on to that, son. We may still need it." He slung a canteen over the pommel of Falwell's horse and another one over Peggy's. "How're you doing?" he asked her.

"Fine, sir, fine," she said.

McHenry flapped the saddlebag with food over the rump of his own horse and then tied it to the saddle.

"Mr. McHenry," Austin whispered, "I hear something."

Turning, McHenry saw the dim silhouette of a figure rise up from the sagebrush and aim a rifle at him.

"Apaches!" he yelled, grabbing his carbine from Austin. The Apache fired before McHenry could bring his weapon to bear. But he missed.

McHenry fired from the hip. The Apache disappeared. McHenry levered in another cartridge and fired again at where the Apache might have gone. The horse next to him leaped up, and McHenry grabbed for the reins, saying, "Whoa, whoa!"

Suddenly other shots rang out. Flashes of light gave away the location of the Apaches.

Falwell fired a shot and shouted, "Let's get out of here!"

Peggy yelped. Her horse reared. She grabbed for the pommel and held on. More shots came from the Apaches. The horse reared again.

Falwell urged his horse in her direction. "Hold him, Miss Winslow!" He reached for the bridle.

The horse shied away from him. An Apache fired from the other side of Peggy. Falwell swung his carbine with one hand and fired at the Apache. Peggy's horse bolted and she cried out in alarm.

The horse charged toward the Apache whom Falwell had shot at. The Apache leaped for Peggy, but the animal galloped past him. Falwell took another shot at the Apache, and the man ducked into the darkness.

"You're going the wrong way!" McHenry shouted at Peggy.

"Mr. McHenry!" Austin shouted. "Behind you!"

McHenry spun around and fired two more quick carbine rounds, though he couldn't tell if he was hitting anything.

Falwell set his horse in motion. "Come on, Mc-Henry!" he shouted behind him. "Hang on, Jeremy!"

Holding the reins, McHenry fired again at one of the flashes of light. "Austin, get up there behind the saddle, boy," he ordered.

Austin leaped for the stirrup, and in a few seconds he was on top of the horse and sitting behind the saddle. He rested the Winchester crosswise right behind the saddle. "I'm up, Mr. McHenry."

McHenry put a boot in the stirrup and hoisted himself

up. He gave the reins a hard tug and kicked the horse with his boots. "Come on, horse!" he shouted. "Go! Hold on tight, Austin."

The fidgeting horse responded instantly. It seemed relieved to be running away from all the gunfire.

McHenry fired once more on the run, but he was pretty sure he didn't hit anything. He drove the horse forward after Falwell, who was racing into the darkness. McHenry followed. "You're going up the canyon, Miss Winslow!" he shouted. He didn't know whether she could hear him, or whether she had control her horse. "We need to go down, not up!"

McHenry's horse ran well, crashing through sagebrush and pounding on the desert floor. Looking back, he saw no flashes of light or claps of gunfire that warned of pursuing bullets. He looked forward again and saw no Apaches shooting from the front, either. "We lost them, Austin," he said. *For the moment, at least*, he thought.

Peggy screamed up ahead. McHenry gave his horse another kick. Then, almost immediately, he heard Jeremy scream. There was a crunch of falling bodies. Now a horse was screaming.

McHenry pulled back on the reins a little. He didn't understand what had happened.

"Watch out, McHenry!" Falwell shouted. "There's a gully up ahead! Our horses are down."

Falwell had not shouted any too soon. McHenry saw him on the ground in a shallow gully. Falwell threw up his arms to ward off what looked like a certain collision. McHenry brought his horse up so hard that it sank to its hindquarters before bouncing up and dancing in a tight circle.

Falwell's horse lay on its side with Falwell still in the saddle and his leg pinned beneath the horse. It looked like the two of them had cartwheeled together into the depression. The horse was not moving.

McHenry could make out Jeremy getting to his feet. He couldn't see Peggy, but her horse was limping in a circle, wheezing and screaming as it tried to walk on a broken leg.

He dismounted quickly, and then Austin slid off the back of the horse and grabbed the reins from him. Holding his Winchester, McHenry jumped down the three-foot embankment, rushed to Falwell's side, and knelt quickly.

"I think it broke its neck," Falwell said. "It's just dead weight on my leg."

McHenry laid the carbine down and tried to roll the horse up a little so Falwell could extract his leg. Falwell gasped in pain. "My leg is broken. I'm sure of it."

McHenry pulled at the horse.

"No," Falwell said, raising a hand. "Help the others first."

McHenry nodded, picked up his carbine, and headed around the fallen horse. "Miss Winslow? Miss Winslow?"

"She's over here," Jeremy called out.

McHenry rushed to her side and knelt down. "How bad are you hurt?" he asked.

She put her hands to her head. "I—I think I just got the wind knocked out of me. I didn't see this hole in the ground." She shook her head to clear it. "Not that I could have stopped the horse."

"It's not a hole but a gully. Water runs down it after the spring rains. It's dry the rest of the year."

Peggy looked in anguish at the horse she had been riding. It was still jumping around in a little circle. Its right front leg stuck out at an odd angle and flopped about as it tried to stand on it. It was whinnying and wheezing in pain.

Austin called to McHenry, "That other horse is making this one nervous."

McHenry stood up and drew his pistol. "I'll take care of that." He went over to the other horse and grabbed its bridle to keep it from pumping its head up and down. He held the horse at arm's length and fired a single bullet into its forehead. The horse dropped like a stone.

Austin yelled as the horse he held whinnied in panic and galloped into the darkness. He fell into the gully and rolled, holding his leg. McHenry ran over to him.

Austin grimaced in pain. "Horse kicked me, Mr. McHenry. I tried to stop him."

McHenry could no longer see the horse racing away. He sighed. "Well, you tried."

"I'm sorry." Austin slowly got to his feet, nursing his wounded leg.

"Can you walk? It's not broken, is it?" McHenry expected the worst.

Austin tried the leg. It held. "No, I'm okay. Just a bad bruise."

"Good. Find your Winchester and take cover behind the gully wall. Keep it pointed in the directions the Apaches will be coming from."

McHenry went back to Peggy. She was standing now, and Jeremy was by her side. "I'm all right," she told him.

"We have to help Falwell," he said. "He's stuck beneath his horse."

All three went over to Falwell, who was breathing heavily. "We'll have to get you out from underneath there," McHenry said. "I'll try to lift the horse while Miss Winslow and Jeremy will help pull you out. Okay?"

Falwell nodded. "Anything is better than this pain." McHenry grabbed the pommel of the saddle. He pulled up as hard as he could. The horse rolled slightly. "Pull him out."

Falwell groaned in pain but he helped push. Peggy grabbed him with both hands under an armpit. Jeremy grabbed the other one. Struggling with his good leg and with the help of the other two people, Falwell managed to pull himself from underneath the horse. He slumped to the ground in relief.

McHenry knelt beside him and touched his leg. "That hurt?"

"Yes. A lot. It's broken."

Peggy touched Falwell's shoulder. "There's no way we can make a splint."

"I know, I know. Just let me rest for a few minutes. What will we do now, McHenry? I can't walk, and we have no horses anymore."

Peggy's shoulders sagged. "It's my fault. I couldn't control that horse."

McHenry sat down with the Winchester across his lap and wiped a hand over his mouth. "Don't blame yourself. We were all in a hurry to get away from the Apaches."

"Where are we now?" Peggy asked.

"We're a lot farther up the canyon than we were before at that first camp," he said. "Those horses covered a lot of ground in a hurry."

"Someone's coming!" Austin cried.

"Drag me over to the wall," Falwell said. He grabbed his Winchester.

"Right." McHenry handed his Winchester to Peggy, grabbed Falwell under the armpits, and dragged him over to the wall. Falwell grimaced the whole time.

McHenry took back his Winchester from Peggy, crouched behind the wall, and peered into the darkness.

"Straight out there," Austin whispered to him.

McHenry stuck the carbine over the top of the gully wall and cocked the hammer. Falwell had his Winchester pointed in the direction the Apaches would come from. Austin had a Winchester too.

Jeremy was not holding a weapon, and McHenry asked where it was.

"Lost it during that ride," the boy reported.

"Could you shoot a pistol?" McHenry asked Peggy.

"I could try."

He drew his pistol and handed it to her. "Just pull the hammer back with your thumbs until it clicks twice to full cock. Then point it at an Apache and pull the trigger."

Peggy nodded.

McHenry went back to studying the darkness. They all fell silent. Then they could hear an occasional crunch of feet.

"Maybe they don't know we're here," Peggy said.

"There they are!" Austin cried, and he fired his Winchester.

Immediately there was an answering yip and yell from the darkness. Guns fired back, flashes of light coming from several places, but all of them from in front.

McHenry and Falwell joined in the firing. Seldom could they see a figure. They just fired at the light flashes.

As the Apache guns fell silent, McHenry held up a hand and said, "I think they withdrew."

Everyone listened. There was no sound in front of them, just a slight breeze through the sagebrush.

He relaxed a little. "I don't think they'll try a front attack again."

Falwell turned and sat back against the dirt wall. "They may circle around us," he said.

McHenry's eyes searched the darkness all the way around the camp. His right hand went to the bandolier for more bullets. His fingers tried every loop on the bandolier. He looked down. Finally he pulled the bandolier over his head and tossed it aside.

"All gone?" Falwell asked.

He nodded, then fingered the loops in his holster belt. Half the loops were empty. He retrieved several cartridges from the belt and slipped them into the carbine.

"I don't have much left," Falwell said.

"How about you, Austin?" McHenry asked.

"I got six bullets left in the Winchester and about that many in my pocket."

"Put them all into the carbine."

"Yes, sir." Austin proceeded to load the weapon.

Falwell shook his head. "It was a trap, and we walked right into it."

McHenry tried to grin. "Guess I was as much taken in as you. Mighty clever of them to herd those horses our way. Mighty clever."

Peggy crawled over to McHenry and asked, "What do we do now?"

"We wait," he answered.

Chapter Ten

"McHENRY!"

McHenry snapped awake into the early dawn just as Falwell's carbine boomed next to him. He fumbled for his own carbine and shook his head to rid it of the cobwebs. He wondered in alarm just when he had fallen asleep.

An Apache was running straight toward the gully from the side McHenry was facing. Still sitting down, McHenry brought the Winchester to his shoulder and fired. But he was still dazed from sleep and he missed. As the Apache swerved, McHenry fired again. The Indian leaped behind a bush and disappeared from view.

Falwell had twisted round and was firing over the embankment in the opposite direction from McHenry. He was levering in cartridges as fast as he could fire them. The empty shell casings plunked onto the ground like rain spatter.

McHenry quickly checked the others. Peggy was awake and had thrown herself against the embankment. Austin had his Winchester pointed in the same direction as Falwell. He was shooting slowly, taking careful aim and working the lever with both hands. Jeremy hugged the wall close to Peggy.

McHenry scanned the desert quickly on both sides of the gully. The Apaches were coming from both directions, and they were already close. They ran a short distance and then dropped out of sight. McHenry hardly had time to get a bead on any of them before they dropped out of sight again. The yelps and screams from the unseen Indians tormented him. "They're like ghosts," he muttered.

"We all fell asleep," Falwell shouted above the blasts of his Winchester. "Lucky we aren't all dead already."

"I haven't hit a single darn one of them so far."

"I got one for sure, and I winged another one." Falwell fired again.

Austin called, "I'm out of ammunition."

McHenry plucked a few cartridges from his gun belt and tossed them over. "Load again, but don't do any more shooting till I tell you. We have to make our ammunition count."

"There must be about a dozen of them," Falwell said.

"How many bullets you got left?"

"Maybe half a dozen in the carbine." Falwell patted his pockets. "Maybe ten or so beyond that."

McHenry reached around and felt the loops in his holster belt. "I'm in about the same shape."

Falwell suddenly snapped up his Winchester and fired.

"Get him?" McHenry asked.

"I don't know. Maybe he was just taking cover. They're not taking chances anymore."

A bullet smacked into the dirt wall behind him. McHenry ducked, then glanced round at their setting. "The canyon's a lot wider here," he said. "Must be over a mile."

"I don't think we'll have to worry about them sniping at us from the cliffs. Too far away."

McHenry nodded. "And it's pretty flat all around here."

Falwell rested his Winchester against the gully wall. "Can't see any right now." He wiped perspiration from his face.

McHenry noticed how much Falwell was sweating though it was not very warm yet. He began to worry even more about him.

"Could you get me a canteen?" Falwell asked.

McHenry retrieved the canteen from Falwell's horse, and the lieutenant drank slowly and appreciatively.

McHenry jiggled the canteen afterward and estimated that it was about half full. "Rest of you want a drink?"

Peggy, Austin, and Jeremy all crawled over quickly.

"Just a couple of swallows," McHenry said. "It's going to get a lot hotter during the day, and we don't have any shade here."

They nodded and took only a short drink. McHenry took a drink too, and the water tasted wonderful.

"I see only two canteens," Peggy said.

McHenry nodded. "I dropped the two canteens I was holding when the Apaches jumped us last night. I didn't pick them up again." Those two canteens would be sorely missed by noon.

"Was the food on the horse that ran off last night?" Falwell asked.

McHenry sighed. "Yeah, the food's gone." He slumped against the gully wall. "It's my fault!"

Austin spoke up: "I'm the one who let the horse get away."

McHenry sighed again. "I should have had you tie the horse down, or taken the saddlebag off before I shot that other horse. I should have—"

"You're being too hard on yourself," Peggy interrupted. "If I'd had control of that horse, we wouldn't be trapped here in this gully in the first place."

"What's done is done," Falwell said. "The only important thing is getting out of here. What do you think, McHenry?"

McHenry wanted to say that he was completely out of ideas. But Peggy was looking hopefully at him. And Austin and Jeremy were eagerly awaiting his reply. He didn't know what to say.

Then, as Apaches began to yell and scream, Falwell started firing again, and McHenry snapped up his carbine and fired in the opposite direction. "Shoot!" he cried to Austin.

The boy plunked the barrel of his Winchester on the embankment, aimed, and fired.

Three Apaches were charging McHenry. He fired three times but missed every shot. His next shot might have hit one of them, but the hammer of his carbine only made a load click when it fell again. He worked the lever, but no cartridge came out. Empty.

He dropped the carbine and drew his pistol. Still kneeling, he used both hands to steady it as he fired at the Indian on the left. The man twisted and tumbled. He drew a bead on the next one. The Apache slid to a stop, raised his Winchester, and fired. The bullet whizzed past McHenry. McHenry fired at him, and the Apache turned and dropped out of sight.

Falwell stopped firing. "Empty!" he shouted. He fumbled in his pocket for more cartridges and poured them out onto the ground. He started shoving them frantically into the carbine's magazine.

The third Apache coming at McHenry slid to a stop and fired his carbine. McHenry fired another bullet and missed.

Falwell grunted and jerked. He dropped his carbine and the cartridges in his hand. He fumbled for the fresh wound in his back and then slid sideways on the dirt wall and rolled slightly as he came to a rest on the ground. He didn't move after that.

McHenry fired his pistol again. The third Apache

turned and ran. He yelped and stumbled. He got to his feet again and continued to run. The second Apache jumped up and took off with him. McHenry fired until the pistol was empty. The two Apaches kept running.

McHenry spun around. He could see several Apaches in the sagebrush.

"Mr. McHenry," Austin shouted, "I'm out of ammunition again!"

McHenry picked up Falwell's carbine and fired. An Apache jumped and ran. He fired again. Now all the Apaches he could see were retreating.

He wiped a hand over his face and tried to catch his breath. He looked back. There were no Apaches visible there, either. He slumped down, but still kept a lookout over the edge of the gully wall.

"Are they gone?" Peggy asked.

He nodded. "I think so." He looked down at Falwell.

"The lieutenant was hit."

Peggy scrambled to her hands and knees and joined McHenry as he bent over Falwell. "He's still alive," he said, looking for the wound. "Took a bullet in the back. Must have been one of the Apaches I didn't hit."

"No reason to blame yourself."

"A week ago I would have hit every one of them."

"We're all exhausted." She tore yet another strip of cloth off her petticoat and then pressed it to Falwell's wound. She let his hands lie at his side. "His body pressure on the cloth will help stem the bleeding."

"I see dust behind us," Austin said.

"Horses on the move," McHenry told him. He scooted over to the other side of the gully and studied the horsemen. "Apaches. They're going up the canyon. Away from us."

Peggy hurried over to him on her hands and knees. She looked over the top of the embankment too. "They're leaving?" she asked. "They're really leaving?"

"You mean we beat 'em off?" Austin asked.

McHenry frowned. "It's more likely that they just decided to head home, but they do seem to be leaving."

Jeremy looked at McHenry. "Does that mean *we* can go home?"

Austin snorted. "And just where is home?" he asked.

"Well, somewhere," Jeremy said weakly.

"We can't be sure that they all left," McHenry murmured.

"Another trick?" Peggy asked.

"Maybe. Or maybe some decided to leave and some didn't. Their leaders lead; they don't command. Depends on how bad the individual Apache wants some prize."

"How do we find out?"

McHenry looked around the gully. He saw sagebrush, cacti, baked yellow dirt, shriveled shrub, a few stunted mesquites, and the canyon walls in the distance. No bird flew, no horse wandered about, hardly a breeze stirred. The sun had reached the gully. There were no Apaches to be seen.

"Guess we just wait," he said. "If there are any Apaches out there, they'll probably just let us cook in the sun for a while." He turned to Austin and asked, "You sure you don't have any more ammunition?"

"I'm positive."

Jeremy scrounged around in his pocket, and then said excitedly, "I got some bullets!"

"That's great. Bring them over here."

Jeremy hurried over to McHenry and offered him a dozen low-caliber cartridges. McHenry looked down at the shiny brass casings and lead bullets. So close, yet so far. "Don't suppose you know where your rifle is, do you, Jeremy?"

Jeremy shook his head and stuck his hand back in his pocket. "Sorry. I didn't think."

McHenry patted him on the back. "It's okay."

McHenry went over to Falwell and checked his pockets, but he had taken out all the cartridges the last time he was reloading. McHenry found seven cartridges on the ground where Falwell had laid them. He then repeatedly worked the lever of Falwell's carbine. Only one cartridge popped out. He reached around and took every cartridge out of his gun belt. There were only five.

McHenry took out his pistol, opened the gate, and jiggled it to help the empty casings fall out. Then he fully reloaded the pistol and put it back in his holster.

He shoved the remaining seven cartridges into the magazine of his own Winchester.

Peggy had been watching him. "That's not many bullets left," she observed with a sigh.

"Thirteen all together," he said. "I'm pretty sure there are fewer than thirteen Apaches out there."

She smiled. "Thanks for the optimism, but I saw how many shots were fired earlier, and how few of the Apaches were hit."

"Yeah. Well, maybe they're all gone, anyway." He stuck his head above the embankment and looked around.

Peggy sat down with her back to the dirt wall. "Maybe, maybe not. What if there's just one Apache out there and he shoots you with just one bullet?" She looked at Austin and Jeremy. They were sitting with their backs to the wall too, but on the other side of the gully, partially hidden by Falwell's dead horse. She asked, "Do you think Austin could really defend the rest of us?"

"Austin's not a bad shot for a boy. Even for a man, for that matter."

Peggy smiled weakly. "He's still just a boy."

McHenry frowned. Her head was bare. "You lost your father's hat," he said.

She put a hand on top of her head. Her hair was hot to the touch. There was no shade in the gully. "It was all I had left of him too. Except memories."

"You won't forget him. Nor will I."

"Thank you, Mr. McHenry."

"In fact, I'm going to name this canyon after him. Winslow Canyon. That way no one will forget him."

She nodded approval. "I would like that. And he would too."

McHenry took off his hat and put it on her head.

She looked up at him. "Don't you need your hat?"

"Not as much as you need it."

She settled it back on her head. "Thank you. It feels good."

"You're welcome." He went back to looking out at the desert. He had to squint now.

"What will the Apaches do to me if they capture me?" Peggy asked.

He couldn't actually tell her. "I won't let them capture you," he promised.

"But you might not be able to stop them. You're only one man. I can't tell you how much I admire you for your courage and all you've done. But you're still just one man."

He sighed. "What I meant was, I won't let them take me alive, and I won't let them take you alive."

Peggy was silent for a moment. "Oh," she said. "Now I understand. It's that horrible, is it?"

"Yes, it is."

She looked over at the two boys. "What about them?"

"Too old already. I wouldn't want the Apaches to capture them alive, either."

"I see. And I won't bother to ask about Lieutenant Falwell."

"It might be best for him if he simply never regained consciousness."

Peggy was silent again for a few moments. "Mr. McHenry, did you ever think that if you hadn't left your ranch, you wouldn't be here in this gully now?"

"Yeah, I guess so. But then," he added, "I wouldn't have met you." After he'd said it, he didn't know why he had blurted that out.

She looked up at him skeptically. "That doesn't really make it worth it, does it?"

He actually laughed. "Well, that remains to be seen." He turned away from the desert and slid down to sit. He looked into her face. It was dirty and burned by the wind, the sand, and the sun. Her hair was unkempt and stuck out from underneath his hat on her head. Her lips were cracked.

"Miss Winslow," he said, "you're the prettiest woman I've ever met. And the nicest, and the, uh—"

She looked at him strangely. "I don't feel pretty right now. Just what kind of thoughts are you having, Mr. McHenry?"

He paused. Finally he pointed to Austin and Jeremy, who had moved back over to the same side of the gully now. "My thoughts are about those boys too," he said.

Peggy glanced at the boys and then back to McHenry. "What?"

"Well, I think I understand Mitch a lot better now.

He says he loves the land, but I think it's his family that makes him feel that way, not the land itself.''

"That makes sense."

McHenry nodded toward the boys. "I can see how Mitch feels so strongly about his own kids. I've been with his kids, of course, and played with them, eaten with them, and so forth. But I've never been responsible for them. And these two boys? Well, I just met them a short time ago, and already I feel like I'm letting them down, that I owed them something. It's—I don't know.''

"It's true, they are attached to you. They took an immediate liking to you."

McHenry smiled. "I picture them on my ranch, helping with the cattle, mending fence, feeding the chickens, eating meals together, sitting on the front porch in the evening, and listening to the nighthawks hunt for insects while I tell them stories. I get such a good feeling when I just pat one of them on the shoulder and call him son." He chuckled and looked down. "That must sound silly to you."

"No, not at all," she said. "In fact, that sounds wonderful."

"I envy your snuggling with them," McHenry said. He smiled.

Peggy smiled too. "Oh?"

"Yeah." He looked at her. "Giving them hugs. They enjoy it so much too."

"Why don't *you* give them a hug? They would love it. In fact, they need it. Particularly right now."

"Ah, it wouldn't seem right. I'm not their father."

"You might as well be. You'd be good at giving hugs."

He laughed quietly.

"In fact," she went on, "most people need hugs at least once in a while. Like right now, for example." She looked up at him.

"Huh?"

"Would you put an arm around me, Mr. McHenry?" she asked. "I'm scared. I'm real scared."

"Well, uh—" He felt like saying he was plenty scared himself, but he didn't think she wanted to hear *that* right now.

"Please?" She slid over to him and rested her head on his shoulder. His hat on her head tilted to one side.

"Well, I guess I could," he said. He slowly lifted his left arm and placed it around her shoulders.

She settled in tighter. "Thank you, sir."

"You're welcome, Miss Winslow." He pulled her a little tighter. Hot as the sun was, it couldn't match the warmth of her body to him.

Peggy spoke again. "Could you take the boys with you when you went back home?"

He frowned. "Home? You mean Chicago?"

"That's not home. Just listen to yourself talk. Chicago can never be home for you. Home is here, just like with Mitch."

"I sold the ranch."

"I heard Mitch say you could have it back, if you wanted it back."

"Well, that's true." McHenry stared into the desert on the other side of the gully. "But it doesn't seem to be something we can think about now."

"Yes, it is. Promise me that you'll take the boys and go back to your ranch."

He smiled weakly, and then he thought about the thirteen bullets he had left. He thought also about the sun hammering them all day. Even now the sun felt like a heavy pressure on his bare head. He lifted a hand and felt how hot his hair and scalp had already become. He thought about sunburn and blistering and how the two dead horses in their midst would stink in a day. He thought about nightfall and the Apaches creeping in. Just thirteen bullets.

Jeremy came running over. He plopped down beside Peggy. "Can I snuggle too?" he asked.

Peggy smiled at him. "Sure, Jeremy." She extended an arm around him, and he smiled and curled up with his head on her shoulder.

McHenry looked down at Peggy and Jeremy. He didn't want to ever move.

"Mr. McHenry," Austin said, crawling closer to him.

McHenry looked over at him. Austin had stopped and was peering over the edge of the embankment.

"Yes, son?" McHenry asked anxiously. And he smiled despite himself. *Son*.

"We're low on ammunition, aren't we?"

McHenry sighed. "I'm afraid so, Austin."

"Well, I see a Winchester lying out there. Maybe it's got some bullets in it."

McHenry unscrambled himself from Peggy and Jeremy. He turned and peered out over the desert.

Austin pointed. "See that cactus between two bushes?"

McHenry followed Austin's hand. There was indeed a Winchester lying in the dirt.

Peggy looked over the top too. "One of the Apaches must have dropped it. Do you think there are bullets in it? Won't they shoot at you if you go out there?"

"Even if there's one bullet in it," McHenry said, "it would be worth snatching." He scanned the desert carefully. "I'm going out there."

"You'll be an easy target," Peggy warned.

"I'm going to move fast, very fast." He studied the carbine lying in the dirt. And then he turned to Peggy. "It's a long way. Still, it's worth a chance. The Apaches won't be expecting me to suddenly leap up and race out there. They may not even be watching right now. Besides, maybe they're all gone."

Peggy frowned deeply. "I think we're about to find out, Mr. McHenry. I wish you wouldn't go out there."

"I'm going." He pulled out his pistol and offered

it to her. "But there's a chance that they're out there, and it's a long way."

Peggy looked up at him, puzzled. "Are you saying you might not come back?"

"If they get me, you mustn't let them get any of you."

She looked at him, horrified.

"There are six bullets in this gun," he explained. "Use no more than two on the Apaches. Then use the remaining four on Falwell, then the boys, and finally yourself."

Peggy shrank back. She opened her mouth and tried to speak, but no words came out.

He shoved the pistol into her hand. He held her fingers around the handle with both of his hands. "Your father said you could do what needed to be done, Miss Winslow. This needs to be done if I don't come back." He stared intently into her eyes. Finally he felt her hand relax.

She nodded. "I understand," she whispered.

"Promise?"

She nodded again. "I promise." She looked over at the boys. They were both looking at her.

Austin swallowed. "We understand too, Miss Winslow," he said. He looked at Jeremy.

Jeremy nodded slowly. "We saw what they did to Pa," Jeremy said quietly.

"If you love us," Austin said, "you'll shoot us before they grab us."

Peggy had tears in her eyes. She tried to smile. She mouthed the word *okay*, but no sound came out. She beckoned with her arms, and the two boys scooted over and they huddled together.

"Okay," McHenry said. He wiped a hand over his mouth and then took a deep breath and let it out slowly. He cocked his Winchester with his thumb. Seven cartridges in the Winchester. "Here I go." He leaped out of the gully and ran.

Chapter Eleven

M c Henry sprinted the whole distance, and with every long stride he expected a shot to ring out. But none came. He reached the carbine and tried to slide to a stop, but he was so eager that he slipped and landed flat on his back next to the Apache Winchester.

He didn't hesitate, though. He grabbed the weapon, leaped to his feet, and broke into a run back toward the gully.

An Apache in dirty white suddenly rose to his knees halfway between McHenry and the gully. The man raised a Winchester and fired, and then just as suddenly dropped back out of sight.

McHenry had dodged to the right violently, and the bullet missed, but he fell again. He rolled, clutching both Winchesters to his chest. He dropped the Apache weapon and brought up his own while still prone.

A clump of sagebrush where the Apache had disappeared moved, and McHenry fired a bullet into it. Nothing stirred.

McHenry no longer had to wonder if there were any

Apaches still around. Now he only wondered how many. He levered another cartridge into the chamber of his Winchester. The empty shell casing plinked onto the ground. One more gone. Six left. He pulled the Apache Winchester closer.

McHenry looked over toward the gully. He could see three hats poking above the gully embankment. So close, yet so far. He wasn't surprised that he'd been shot at, but it hadn't occurred to him that the Apaches would be in between him and Peggy and the others. He had to get back to the gully.

He rolled over quickly to the next sagebrush. There was also a small clump of cacti nearby. He searched the desert in front of him. He thought it unlikely that the Apache would stay put. However, the Apache had the advantage of knowing that McHenry wanted to get back to the gully. McHenry decided to take the long way around, which might confuse the Apache.

He grabbed both Winchesters and leaped to his feet. He ran a mere twenty feet before plopping down again. The Apache was going to know immediately he had moved. If the Apache got up to follow, McHenry wanted to be ready. He brought up his Winchester and waited.

No Apache appeared. No shots came. McHenry looked all around. He had no way of knowing how many Apaches there were in the area. He could be surrounded and not know it. Perhaps the Apache was crawling toward him. As he studied the desert, he was amazed how such sparse vegetation could actually provide so much cover. Even though he would be as shielded from view from the Apache as the Apache was from him, the Apache would know where he had just dropped down.

McHenry rested the Apache Winchester across his arms and slithered forward, keeping his own gun in his hands and cocked.

He stopped. Still no sign of the Apache. And he couldn't see the gully from here, either. Then he heard scratching off to his right. The Apache was crawling too, staying in between him and the gully.

He turned his attention in that direction. He tried to calm himself so that the blood pounding in his ears wouldn't affect his hearing. He squinted in the bright sunlight. He sorely missed his hat.

He waited, now regretting the earlier shot. It had been wasted, fired in panic at a target he couldn't see. He would be careful this time.

He heard movement to his left and twisted about. His eyes widened and he sucked in his breath. He could see an Apache lying behind some sagebrush. But this one was wearing a tan tunic whereas the one who had shot at him before had been in white.

McHenry brought the Winchester around. The Apache had moved a bit by the time he got a bead on him. He could make out only the vague color through the brush. He aimed carefully and fired. The Apache yelped and jumped up. McHenry worked the lever of his Winchester, but before he could take aim again, the Apache had dropped out of sight.

McHenry let out a breath slowly. He was sure he had hit the man, but it hadn't been fatal. Five cartridges left.

Peggy screamed. Then McHenry heard the pistol he had given her. And Austin was shouting, "Mr. McHenry! Mr. McHenry!"

McHenry couldn't see the gully from where he was lying now. He had no choice. He rose to his knees and looked.

Two Apaches were charging toward the gully from the other side. Peggy had stood up and was holding the pistol with both hands as she pointed it toward the two Apaches rushing toward her. She fired again. A miss. While McHenry watched, and before he could react, she fired yet another time.

"No!" he gasped. "That's three times. You've only got three bullets left."

He brought the Winchester up. He fired. Missed. Four left.

Peggy covered her head. She spun around and saw McHenry. She dropped out of sight behind the gully wall.

McHenry levered in another cartridge. He fired again. Another miss. Three left.

He worked the lever again. He couldn't believe he had missed a shot that would have been easy just a couple of days ago. It was because of the heat, the lack of food and water, and the fear. He brought up a foot so he could rest his elbow on his knee. He aimed once more. He fired.

An Apache spun around and dropped to the ground. McHenry levered one of his two remaining cartridges into the chamber. The other Apache slid to a stop, grabbed the downed Apache, and helped him to his feet. Together they sprinted away.

McHenry aimed at their backs. He debated. Should he try another shot with only two cartridges left? He didn't know how many rounds were in the Apache carbine he had with him. He should have checked immediately. But one less Apache was one less Apache, and their backs presented broad, easy targets. He fired.

He shouldn't have debated so long. It had allowed them too much distance. His shot missed. He snarled at himself and levered his last cartridge into the chamber of his Winchester.

He reached down to pick up the Apache Winchester and was getting up when the Apache in dirty white leaped to his feet not ten feet away and rushed screaming toward him with a knife held high in one hand.

McHenry jumped in fright, dropped the Apache Winchester, and swung his own around. The Apache collided with him and the carbine fired. They both toppled over, and the Apache drove the knife into McHenry's shoulder.

McHenry yelled in pain. With his Winchester he

heaved the Apache off of him. The Apache rolled away and McHenry rolled in the opposite direction. The Apache jumped to his feet and charged again. McHenry worked the lever of his Winchester, brought the gun to bear, and pulled the trigger. Nothing. Empty.

He rolled again as the Apache leaped and brought the knife down. The knife sliced through the back of McHenry's vest and shirt and tore a gash through his flesh over his ribs.

McHenry gasped. He rolled and rolled and came up on his knees as the Apache attacked again. The Apache threw himself at McHenry and knocked him back off his knees. As the Indian tumbled over McHenry, he slashed at him with his knife. The blade caught McHenry in the side. The Indian tumbled to the ground beyond him.

McHenry grimaced and rolled. He was slower getting up this time and made it only to his knees before the Apache was on him again. McHenry swung the Winchester by the barrel and cracked the Apache's knee. The Indian twisted and went down.

McHenry staggered to his feet. He raised the Winchester like a club and brought it down. The Apache dodged and lunged with the knife. McHenry leaped back and fell down, dropping the carbine and grunting from the pain in his wounds. He knew he was losing. He knew that the Apache was enjoying this kill, slow and playful, a slice at a time.

The Apache yelled and leaped on top of McHenry.

McHenry caught his knife hand with his left hand and he grabbed the Apache by the throat with his right. The Indian thrashed his head about, and he clawed at McHenry's face with his free hand.

McHenry heard Peggy yelling, "Jason!" as he and the Apache rolled. He saw Peggy running toward him, skirts flying, his hat gone, the pistol still gripped tightly in both her hands.

"Get back, Peggy!" he yelled.

He and the Apache rolled and rolled, crunching sagebrush and prickly pear. The Apache wound up on top again, and he shifted both hands to the knife and put his body weight behind it. McHenry grunted and pushed back with both hands.

"Jason!" The call was nearer.

"Go back, Peggy!" McHenry shouted.

McHenry lunged to the side, and the two men rolled once more. But once more the Indian came out on top, and once more the weight of the man forced the knife point closer to McHenry's throat.

A shot exploded a few feet from the two men, and dirt spouted next to them. Both men jumped. McHenry's head twisted.

"Peggy!" he shouted. "No."

The Apache wrenched himself free from McHenry's grip and rolled away. McHenry let him go and collapsed. Peggy took a couple of steps after the Apache as she cocked the hammer again with both thumbs.

"Peggy, wait," McHenry blurted. He tried to get up.

Peggy's pistol shook and swayed as she tried to draw another bead. Finally she fired. The Apache yelped as the slug tore into his arm.

Peggy had the gun cocked again. She pointed and grimaced as she pulled the trigger again. The blast knocked the Apache off his feet and he landed on his back and lay still.

Peggy rushed up to the motionless Apache and pointed the pistol at the man's chest and pulled the trigger. Click. She pulled the trigger again. Click.

"It's empty." McHenry sighed as he slowly got to his feet. His wounds hurt.

Peggy rushed to his side and grabbed his arm. She still held the pistol with her other hand. "You're hurt, Jason," she said.

"They're not deep." He tried to straighten up, but that sent a sharp pain through his side. "Lot of blood maybe, but I'll make it."

"Let me look." She started to examine the wound on his side.

"Not now," he said and then pointed to the pistol. "You used up all six cartridges."

"I couldn't let that man kill you, Jason," she explained. "I just couldn't."

"But he's not the only one out here, Peggy."

"Did you think I could just watch?"

"Well. . . ." Then he smiled. "I guess not. Anyway," he went on, stooping down very slowly for the two carbines, "there'll be some cartridges in this Apache carbine."

Peggy tried to use her free hand to support him. "We have to get back to the gully right away," she said, looking anxiously at the surrounding desert.

He nodded. "But first help me find the carbine the Apache you shot must have had. He probably left it right where he jumped up from." He strode over to where he thought the Apache had come from. But no carbine lay there.

Peggy tugged at his arm. "We can't stay out here, Jason. The other Apaches may attack."

"We have to find that carbine. I'm out of ammunition except for what's in this other Apache carbine."

A shot rang out. They both turned. The Apache in tan had just fired at them, and he was levering another cartridge into his Winchester. He was far off to the left, however.

"Go! Go!" McHenry cried. "Back to the gully! Hurry!"

They both ran. Another shot hurried them on their way. They reached the gully and leaped to its floor. They both tumbled. McHenry sucked in his breath at the pain. Austin and Jeremy helped them to their knees.

"Now I'll look at those wounds, Jason," Peggy said.

McHenry nodded. He looked back across the desert,

but the Apache in tan had disappeared. "Boys, you keep a sharp lookout," he said.

"Yes, sir."

"Lie down," Peggy told him.

"Yes, ma'am." He put the two Winchesters down first and then lay down on his stomach. "Ow."

Peggy once more went to her petticoat and tore three long strips of cloth from it. She started packing the cloth into the wound on McHenry's back. "It's a long wound, Jason," she said, "but it's not deep."

"Yeah." He flinched as the cloth touched the open wound.

Finished with that wound, she ordered, "Roll on your good side."

He rolled over and lifted his arm. She tore his shirt open on the side so she could get at the wound there.

"This one's deeper," she said anxiously. "You're losing a lot of blood."

"I'll be all right," he assured her. While she worked at the wound, he said, "You've been calling me Jason."

She paused in her work and looked at him. "Why, so I have." She resumed working. Then she stopped again. "And you called me Peggy," she pointed out.

"You called me Jason before I called you Peggy," he said.

She smiled a bit. "What do you suppose that means?" she asked.

He looked at her face with the hot sun burning into

it. He reached up and gently touched her cheek with his fingertips.

She stopped working. Her hand slowly rose to touch the back of his hand. She looked at him. There was sadness in her eyes.

He let his hand back down. "Peggy," he said, "I didn't finish that little story I was telling you."

"What story was that?" she asked. She went back to work on the wound in his side.

"The story about me on the porch with the boys."

"What was missing?"

He hesitated, then took a deep breath and said, "*You* were. I want you on that porch with us."

Peggy looked at him again. She smiled. "Let's look at that shoulder wound now."

"Your looks don't tell everything about you, Peggy," McHenry said. He rolled over on his back again. He gasped as the ground pressed up against his wound. "You can be tough when you have to be."

She pressed a cloth strip against the knife wound in his shoulder. "It's a hard country, Jason. Like you've said."

He gritted his teeth at the touch of the cloth on the open wound. "Yes, but you're hard enough to survive out here. But maybe you're right when you say this country is *too* hard. And I know I'm right when I say that you have a softness to you that this country needs."

Peggy finished with the bandage.

"Come back home with me, Peggy Winslow," McHenry said. "Be my wife."

Peggy's mouth dropped opened in surprise at his last words. Then she slowly closed it. She reached over and ran her fingers through his hair. "We are living in a world of make-believe," she said. Then she slowly bent over and kissed him lightly on the lips.

He knew what she meant. They were stranded in the middle of a desert canyon surrounded by Apaches, and with no help expected. Maybe there was no future at all, much less a future together.

Ammunition. He sat straight up, ignoring the resulting pain.

"What's wrong?" Peggy asked. "Did you hear something?"

He shook his head. "The Apache carbine. Have to find out how many rounds we have."

Still sitting, he grabbed the carbine and worked the lever once. An empty shell casing popped out. He looked at Peggy. "Count them," he said.

She nodded.

He worked the lever again. Nothing. Frantically he worked the lever another six times. No cartridges ejected.

His eyes were wide when he looked at Peggy. She put trembling fingers to her lips.

"We have no bullets at all, do we?" she said.

He snarled, lifted the carbine over his head, and then

hurled it against the far dirt wall of the gully. His fists clenched and then relaxed. He looked slowly at Peggy.

"No," he said. "We're completely out of ammunition."

Chapter Twelve

M CHENRY slowly opened his eyes. Then he jerked his head up. "Peggy?"

Peggy put a fingertip to his lips. "I'm here," she said. In fact, she had her head on his shoulder and her arm across his chest as they lay on the ground. "You've been sleeping."

As he got up on his elbows, she raised her head. He flinched at the pain in his back and his side and his shoulder. When he moved his body, he could feel the blood that had soaked down into his trousers. And his whole body was soaked in sweat.

He looked around. Austin was peering over the dirt wall, and Jeremy was sitting near Austin and setting up shell casings in little rows.

McHenry squinted at the sun. It was getting low in the sky. "I must've been sleeping a long time."

"You're weak from all the blood you've lost," Peggy reminded him.

He looked over at Falwell. "How's the lieutenant?"

"His pulse is very weak." She leaned closer and

whispered, ''Why do you suppose the Apaches haven't attacked us again?''

He shrugged. ''They don't know we're out of ammunition. And I'll kick 'em to death if I have to.'' He smiled weakly.

''My dear Jason.'' Peggy smiled too.

''I've been thinking, Peggy. Tonight I'm going to crawl out there and try to get a gun away from one of those Apaches.''

She put her head back down on his shoulder. She didn't say anything.

''I suppose you think that I don't have a chance, huh?'' he said. Frankly, he didn't think he did, either.

''I doubt you could walk very far, much less fight an Apache to the death with your bare hands.''

He was silent. He couldn't talk about the other plans he was working on. Such as how to kill all of them without a gun. How could he do it? Strangle them? Hit them with a rock? He just couldn't let the Apaches capture them alive.

''Mr. McHenry,'' Austin said, ''I see riders.''

Jeremy spilled the shell casings and went to the wall to look.

McHenry shuddered inwardly. More Apaches. ''Coming back down the canyon?'' he asked. He started to get up. Peggy pulled back from him and tried to support his back with her hands.

''No, they're already down the canyon,'' Austin reported.

"Let's see." McHenry got to his hands and knees and crawled over to the embankment. His head spun with dizziness and he could hardly move his limbs. He peered cautiously over the edge, dreading what he was about to see.

"Down there, Mr. McHenry," Austin said. "See 'em?"

"Yes, I see them." McHenry squinted. Then he rubbed his eyes with both hands and looked again. "Peggy! Peggy!" he cried. "Look!"

Peggy got to her hands and knees and came over to the dirt wall. She looked over the edge toward where he was pointing. Far down the canyon a column of riders could be seen. Even at this distance their blue uniforms were unmistakable.

"Cavalry, Peggy!" McHenry said. He was grinning. "That's Mitch in front with the detachment commander. He found the patrol Falwell was talking about."

Peggy actually giggled. "The Army?"

"Yes, soldiers. Must be ten or twelve of them."

Peggy started to smile too, but then she stopped. "But they're turning the wrong way, Jason," she said.

"Huh?" McHenry looked back at the column. They definitely had turned back down the canyon.

"Where they goin'?" Austin asked. He sounded very worried.

"Don't they see us?" Jeremy asked.

McHenry wet his lips. "No, they don't. They don't

know we're up this way. They must be where we had the first fight with the Apaches. We went back down the canyon from there, not up. They're just following our tracks.''

''Will they come back this way?'' Peggy asked. ''Soon?''

''When they get to where we got on those horses, they may not be able to figure out what happened, and just keep going out, thinking they must have passed us somewhere outside the canyon. Mitch is no tracker. He's just a rancher. And soldiers have trouble finding their way to a blazing campfire in the dark.'' He wiped a hand over his face.

''We have to signal them,'' Peggy said. ''We have to let them know we're up here, not down there.''

McHenry watched the column stir up dust. The cloud obscured his vision of the cavalrymen. He breathed faster. Finally he just shouted ''Mitch!'' at the top of his lungs.

The others took his cue. ''Help! Mitch! Soldiers! We're up here!'' The boys actually screamed.

The column kept going.

''They can't hear us,'' Peggy said. ''They're going away.''

''They'd hear a shot, I'll bet,'' McHenry said.

''We don't have any bullets,'' Peggy reminded him.

McHenry scanned the nearby desert. ''No, but they do.''

''Who? The Apaches?'' Peggy asked. ''Well, they

sure aren't going to want to attract the Army's attention.''

"I could make them," McHenry said. "Make them fire a shot."

"How?"

"I'm going to attack them."

"Jason!"

He turned toward her. "What other chance do we have?" He turned back toward the column. "Within a few minutes they won't even hear a gunshot. And at dusk the Apaches will probably attack and—" He didn't finish the thought.

"Please don't go out there, Jason," Peggy begged. "I couldn't bear it."

"I have to."

"No, please, don't!" She threw her arms around him.

He flinched from the resulting pain in his wounds. "I have to because—"

"Because why?" Peggy asked. She squeezed him more tightly.

"Because I love you, Peggy Winslow," he said. He put an arm around her. "I love you."

Peggy squeezed again. "And I love you, Jason McHenry."

He broke from the embrace. Reluctantly, Peggy let go of him. He grabbed his Winchester and stood up.

"Jason, there are no bullets in that gun," she said.

"The Apaches don't know that."

Austin and Jeremy came running over. "You going to get the soldiers, Mr. McHenry?"

McHenry used his free hand to squeeze the shoulder of each of the boys. "See you later, son," he told one and then the other.

Peggy got to her feet. She reached out and touched McHenry's sleeve. "Good luck, Jason."

He smiled at her. "Thanks, Peggy."

He climbed up on the embankment, holding the Winchester in both his hands across his chest. "Mitch!" he called. As he started jogging forward, he could feel each of his wounds split open anew and warm blood seep out. "Mitch, we're back here!" He broke into a full run. "Mitch!" he screamed.

An Apache rose off to his right. The man was a considerable distance away. He raised a carbine and fired.

McHenry ducked and kept running. "Missed me!" he called. "Try again! Shoot! *Shoot!*" He could see that the cavalry patrol had not stopped or turned.

The Apache fired again. The second shot also missed.

McHenry kept running, faster now, all out. "Mitch!"

The Apache fired a third time. This time the bullet caught McHenry in the lower side near the knife wound. He felt as if someone had taken a big club and swung it with all his might to hit him. He spun around and crashed to the ground.

"Mitch?" He looked toward the column. But his eyes wouldn't focus. "Please, Mitch," he said, but it was barely a whisper. And then the horizon turned upside down and everything went black.

Chapter Thirteen

M C HENRY could see only blue. Deep blue. Not like sky. He blinked slowly. A blue uniform. Kneeling next to him while he lay on the ground.

"Mr. McHenry?" the man in the uniform said.

"Jason?" Peggy asked. She was wiping down his face with a cloth dripping with water. It tasted good when it trickled into his mouth.

McHenry looked at her. "Peggy," he said. "They came."

She nodded. "They heard the shots."

"Jason, I didn't think you'd ever wake up," another voice said. It was Mitch.

McHenry smiled. "You old buzzard," he said. "You found them."

"I said I would. You young folks just got no confidence in people older than you."

McHenry reached up a hand. "Thanks, Mitch. Thanks more than you'll ever know."

"Oh, I think I know plenty." Mitch winked at him.

The cavalry captain spoke again: "There were only a few Apaches left, Mr. McHenry, and they took off like rabbits as soon as they saw us coming. We'd have chased them, but it sounds like they took quite a beating from you people already, and we need to get you and Lieutenant Falwell to a doctor as quick as we can.''

McHenry just nodded slightly.

''I've sent some men back to the stage station to get some fence poles. They're going to make a travois for each of you. And I've also dispatched a courier to have an ambulance sent as quickly as possible. Both of you men have lost a lot of blood, but I'm sure you'll pull through.'' Gently, the officer touched McHenry on the shoulder. ''You'll be okay.''

''Thanks,'' McHenry said.

The captain stood up and walked toward some of his men, who were trying to get the saddles off the dead horses.

McHenry saw Austin peering at him over Peggy's shoulder. The boy was chewing vigorously on some beef jerky. ''How are you, son?'' McHenry asked.

Austin swallowed. ''I'm fine, Mr. McHenry.''

Jeremy came running up. ''They've got cheese too, Mr. McHenry!'' he cried. ''And biscuits and plenty of water! It all tastes great!''

McHenry smiled.

Austin looked over Peggy's shoulder. ''Mr. McHenry, the captain says he doesn't know what's going to happen to Jeremy and me. Where are we going?''

Jeremy peered over Peggy's shoulder too. ''Can't we stay with you, Mr. McHenry? Please?''

McHenry looked at Peggy. "You never did answer my question," he reminded her. "Do I go on to Chicago, or should we all go back to my ranch?"

She smiled at him. "Let's go home, Jason," she said. "Let's all go home."

Now he smiled too. "You heard her, boys," he said.

"Yippee!" Austin and Jeremy started dancing a jig.

McHenry started to laugh, but a sharp pain shot through his side, and he gasped and his back stiffened.

Peggy frowned in concern and squeezed his hand. "It must hurt bad," she said.

McHenry squeezed back. His smile returned and his body relaxed again. "No," he told her. "In fact, I've never felt this good in my whole life."